The Murder of
Shakespeare's
Ghost

Seaview Cottages Cozy Mystery #2

Anna Celeste Burke

Books by USA Today and Wall Street Journal Bestselling Author
Anna Celeste Burke

A Dead Husband Jessica Huntington Desert Cities Mystery #1

A Dead Sister Jessica Huntington Desert Cities Mystery #2

A Dead Daughter Jessica Huntington Desert Cities Mystery #3

A Dead Mother Jessica Huntington Desert Cities Mystery #4

A Dead Cousin Jessica Huntington Desert Cities Mystery #5

A Dead Nephew Jessica Huntington Desert Cities Mystery #6 [2019]

Love A Foot Above the Ground Prequel to the Jessica Huntington Desert Cities Mystery Series

Cowabunga Christmas! Corsario Cove Cozy Mystery #1

Gnarly New Year! Corsario Cove Cozy Mystery #2

Heinous Habits! Corsario Cove Cozy Mystery #3

Radical Regatta! Corsario Cove Cozy Mystery #4

Murder at Catmmando Mountain Georgie Shaw Cozy Mystery #1

Love Notes in the Key of Sea Georgie Shaw Cozy Mystery #2

All Hallows' Eve Heist Georgie Shaw Cozy Mystery #3

A Merry Christmas Wedding Mystery Georgie Shaw Cozy
Mystery #4

Murder at Sea of Passenger X Georgie Shaw Cozy
Mystery #5

Murder of the Maestro Georgie Shaw Cozy Mystery #6

A Tango Before Dying Georgie Shaw Cozy Mystery #7

A Canary in the Canal Georgie Shaw Cozy Mystery #8
[2019]

A Body on Fitzgerald's Bluff Seaview Cottages Cozy
Mystery #1

The Murder of Shakespeare's Ghost Seaview Cottages
Cozy Mystery #2

Grave Expectations on Dickens' Dune Seaview Cottages
Cozy Mystery #3 [2019]

Lily's Homecoming Under Fire Calla Lily Mystery #1

Tangled Vines, Buried Secrets Calla Lily Mystery #2
[2019]

DEDICATION

To fans of the "The Bard of Avon," a poet, playwright, and actor whose life remains shrouded in mystery. They say his ghost still walks the streets of Avon.

Contents

Acknowledgments

Thank you to my husband who's support for my writing never falters.

Thanks, as well, to Peggy Hyndman who always has more going on than any woman I know. Somehow, she still finds time to squeeze my books into her queue for editing. I wish I could learn to leave more wiggle room, but I always seem to be running up against a deadline. Thank you, Peggy!

I'm also grateful to Ying Cooper for taking a second look at this manuscript, even though I keep her busy as the first editor on two other series I write. She's also incredibly gracious under fire when the deadline is closing fast and furiously.

I can't miss this opportunity to express my gratitude, once again, to my readers for their ongoing support. That's especially true for my "ARC Angels" who read imperfect versions of my books before they're published and cheer me on! I'm blessed by their feedback and encouragement.

Cast of Characters

Dear reader, if you'd prefer to be surprised as each character is introduced please skip this section!

GRAND OLD LADY DETECTIVES:

Miriam Webster, who lives in Hemingway Cottage, was a bookkeeper, is a talented baker, and her fur baby is a Dalmatian, named Domino. Domino discovered the body behind Fitzgerald's Bluff.

Penelope Parker lives in Brontë Cottage, is a member of the Seaview Cottages Walkers Club, and has a Jack Russell terrier, named Emily. Penelope prefers to be called Charly in honor of her favorite writer, Charlotte Brontë, and is a retired criminology professor.

Cornelia "Neely" Conrad lives in Christie Cottage and is a self-proclaimed night owl who loves to read. Neely is retired and was an actress, turned costume designer and makeup artist.

Marty Monroe lives in Fitzgerald Cottage and is a member of the Seaview Cottages Walkers Club. Before retiring, Marty spent decades working as a buyer for high-end department stores.

Midge Gaylord lives in Austen Cottage and is a member of the Seaview Cottages Walkers Club. Midge is an ex-Army trauma care nurse, with ties to the local medical community.

OTHER SEAVIEW COTTAGES RESIDENTS AND EMPLOYEES:

Carl Rodgers lives in Steinbeck Cottage and is the former manager of a collection agency.

Greta Bishop lives in Garbo Cottage and used to be the resident Realtor and a Seaview Cottages HOA board member until legal issues led to her resignation.

Joe Torrance, who lives in Chandler Cottage, is a retired auto dealership service manager and mechanic.

Robyn Chappell rents Shakespeare Cottage.

Rosemary Pfeiffer is the receptionist for Seaview Cottages Community Clubhouse.

Dottie Harris is Charly's neighbor who lives in the O'Connor Cottage.

LAW ENFORCEMENT:

Darnell Devers is a Deputy Sheriff who all the locals have various pet names for due to his "do as little as possible attitude."

Henry "Hank" Miller is the personable and competent lead detective assigned to investigate the death of Diana Durand.

Eddie Vargas is a detective from outside the local area who's working with Hank Miller.

Neve is an investigator from the County Coroner's Office.

Sabina is a Crime Scene Investigator.

SECONDARY CHARACTERS:

Ted De Voss is the owner of Shakespeare Cottage and a member of the family that used to own all the property on which the Seaview Cottages Community was built.

Bernadette "Bernie" De Voss is Ted De Voss's wife.

Daniel De Voss is the deceased brother of Ted De Voss.

Constance "Cookie" De Voss was Daniel De Voss's wife.

Danny De Voss is Ted De Voss's son.

George Pierson is the landlord who manages the rental of Shakespeare Cottage for the De Voss family.

Mickey Paulson is a local resident of Duneville Down with a criminal record.

1

Be Cruel to be Kind

"I must be cruel only to be kind."
—Hamlet

∞

"H E'S HERE," THE voice whispered when I answered my phone.

"Who's where?" I asked as I glanced at the time and tried to wake up. It was almost midnight. I must have dozed off while reading. I was sitting in my comfy chair in the great room long after my usual bedtime.

"Shakespeare's ghost. He's in my hallway."

"Robyn? It is you, isn't it?" Why did I ask? Who else could it be besides Robyn Chappell, the skittish resident of the Shakespeare Cottage in the Writers' Circle at Seaview Cottages?

"Yes," she whispered. "Please hurry! I'm scared. I'm locked in my bedroom, but ghosts can pass through walls, can't they?" My heart rate sped up. The terror in her voice reached out and grabbed me over the phone. I don't believe in ghosts, but real people scare me. They can pick locks or break down doors—if someone was in Robyn's cottage.

"I'm on my way! Don't wait for me to get there. Call security and the police."

"You know they won't do anything. They've already told me I'm crazy, Miriam. That's why I hired G.O.L.D. to help me." By G.O.L.D., she meant the Grand Old Lady Detectives group my friends and I had formed after a murder on the bluffs had propelled us into the role of amateur sleuths.

"I'll call Charly and have her join me along the way. We'll get to you as soon as we can—probably before the police or security have a chance to respond. Notify them anyway. If there's an intruder in your home, someone in authority needs to take the person into custody."

"It's not a person. It's a ghost—Shakespeare's ghost!" Robyn's whisper had become a hoarse one.

"Don't tell the 911 dispatcher it's a ghost—just say intruder, okay?" I'd already thrown on a coat over my pajamas and slipped on a pair of shoes.

"You don't believe me either, do you? Joe and Carl said you would!"

"I believe something is going on which is why I'm already on my way. It's also why I want you to stay in your bedroom with the door locked. Don't open it until you're sure it's me."

"Call me when you get here," Robyn whispered. "I can hear him! I'm going to hide in the back of my closet." Then she ended the call before I could tell her the reception in her closet might not be great.

I grabbed the large heavy-duty flashlight that was stored in the laundry room and gave it a swing. It could do some damage—to a person, anyway—if I could bring myself to use it. The prospect of whacking an intruder over the head was unappealing. Not as unappealing, however, as allowing someone to attack Robyn or Charly or me. A line from Shakespeare's Hamlet escaped from my lips.

"'*I must be cruel only to be kind*,'" I muttered as I checked to make sure the beam came on. "At least I'll be able to see the dirt bag coming if it's a mere mortal skulking about in the Shakespeare Cottage." As I called Charly on my phone, I grabbed Domino's leash and hollered.

"Domino! Come!" My sweet, sensitive Dalmatian would know better than any of us if someone was in Robyn's home.

"Charly," I said when the ringing stopped, and I heard a groggy grunt on the other end of the phone. "It's me, Miriam. Robyn just called. She says she has an uninvited visitor in her cottage." I gave her the two-sentence version of what that meant.

"How can that be? When we did a walkthrough a few days ago, we checked all the locks on her doors and windows. Everything appeared to be in working order. Did the intruder set off the alarm on her security system?" Emily, the Jack Russel Terrier who lives with Charly in the Brontë Cottage, yipped in the background.

"I didn't ask, although I can't believe she wouldn't have mentioned it, especially when I told her to call security and the police. An intruder would have automatically triggered a response from security—unless it is Shakespeare's ghost as Robyn claims."

"Leash, Emily!" Emily yelped enthusiastically when

she heard Charly utter that command.

"Or unless she forgot to set it before she went to bed. I'm throwing on some clothes. Emily and I will meet you out front as soon as you and Domino can get here."

"We're already outside!" I hadn't stopped moving as I spoke to Charly on the phone, so Domino and I had left the house. I shut the front gate to the Hemingway Cottage where we live, and we hustled along the sidewalk toward Charly's house.

I glanced warily from side-to-side. Most of the lights were out in my neighbors' cottages, but the street lights were on. I didn't need the flashlight to see where I was going in this section of the Writers' Circle. The gentle breeze coming in off the Pacific Ocean beyond the bluffs below us caused everything around us to rustle. Shadows danced. I tightened my grip on the makeshift weapon in my hand.

Domino was delighted to be out at such an hour and was pulling at her leash despite the brisk pace I'd already set. Most of our walks take place in the wee hours of the morning. Years working as a bookkeeper in a bakery had turned me into a morning person. Domino is so smart, I'm sure her urgency was because we were on our way to Emily's cottage. My Dalmatian, who won't be a year old for another month, has forty pounds on the spunky little Jack Russel Terrier with whom she'd formed a solid doggy friendship.

As we rushed along the familiar path, I huffed and puffed. Thank goodness I'd renewed my commitment to exercise, or it would have been worse. An image of Hank Miller flitted through my mind. I'd met the attractive fifty-something homicide detective during the investigation into the murder of a woman on Fitzgerald's Bluff. Lately, his face popped up at the oddest moments. I shut out the idea that my renewed devotion to exercise had anything to do with his smile or the twinkle in his blue eyes.

Stop it! I chided myself. As far as Hank Miller knows, I'm Mrs. Miriam Webster, a married woman with no interest in good-looking men with blue or any other color eyes. In truth, as a newly widowed woman too young to reside in the community without my age-qualified spouse, I'd done what I could to conceal my age and new status as a widow to everyone. Thanks to Charly and members of the homeowners' association board where I'm on the Finance Committee, the problem has been solved. I have no idea how I can ever correct Hank's misperception without confessing that I'd spent my first few months at Seaview Cottages living in a cloud of lies.

"Fitness is important, isn't it? You never know when you'll need to run for it, do you, girl?" Domino glanced over her shoulder at me without slowing down. I took her silence to mean she agreed with me. The fact that she wasn't spooked ought to be reassuring, but it wasn't. I flinched at the keening of a Killdeer overhead and pressed on.

Before I could see her, I heard Emily's excited greeting. I sighed with relief at the welcome sound that had grown so familiar since Domino and I moved into the Hemingway Cottage. It was even more reassuring to hear Charly speak.

"Shush, Emily!" Charly commanded in a firm, low voice as we arrived at their gate. "We don't want to wake up Dottie. She's not feeling well." I put my finger to my lips as we all stood in a pool of light from a streetlamp. That kept Domino from launching into an audible response to Emily's yelps. They settled for wiggles of excitement and tail-wagging as Charly and Emily joined us on the sidewalk.

"Is Dottie Harris sick?" I asked. Dottie is Charly's neighbor in the O'Connor Cottage. The two women in their seventies look out for each other as do many residents in our active adult community.

"Not really. She pulled a muscle in her back trying to power wash her fence. Dottie will be fine if Emily doesn't wake her and she can sleep it off." Charly spoke again as she pointed to my flashlight and closed the gate behind her. "That's a good idea."

"It's the first thing I saw that seemed sturdy enough to use as a weapon." Charly nodded.

"Good choice! I'm armed, too," she said as she held up her keychain. Even in the low light that enveloped us, she must have been able to read the skeptical expression on my face. "Don't be deceived. It's a kubotan."

"What's a kubotan?" I asked.

"Essentially it's a mini-stick for self-defense. The kubotan keychain is based on a small bamboo weapon called the 'hashi stick.' A famous martial arts master, Kubota, developed it when the Los Angeles Police Department asked him to create a self-defense weapon and train officers to use it. It's really quite effective if you skillfully apply it to vulnerable spots on an assailant's body." With lightning quick speed Charly, whose background included training in jiu-jitsu, made a couple of stabbing motions and then repositioned her grip on the keychain and the kubotan became a mini-flail. In another instant, the kubotan keychain had virtually vanished from sight, palmed in Charly's hand hanging at her side.

"Well, I'm glad you're with me. I obviously brought something to wield against a bad guy, but I don't trust my ability to use it with skill or conviction."

"Once a bad guy or two has acted with conviction toward you, it becomes less objectionable." Charly grew silent for a moment as if wrestling with an old memory, perhaps tied to the reason she'd mastered jiu-jitsu. She's retired now, but Charly had a distinguished career as a criminology professor and taught courses at the police academy. The memorabilia from her travels hinted there was more to her past. A photo or two that I'd glimpsed in her home office somehow conveyed that not all her trips were holiday junkets. "You've made me realize that we ought to spend a little time honing our self-defense skills before we take on more clients. We already have a second request for assistance, by the way."

"Are you kidding? It's not another haunting, is it?" We'd rounded the corner and were about to step off the curb when Charly and I stopped dead in our tracks. That might not have been the best choice of words under the circumstances. "What is that?"

2

Cold Comfort

"I do not ask you much, I beg cold comfort;
and you are so strait and so ingrateful, you deny
me that."

—King John

∞

A GLOWING WHITE form emerged from the bushes across the street, catty-cornered to us. The figure came from out of nowhere near the Shakespeare Cottage and darted toward a small parklike area, still across the street, but closer to us. Then the motion stopped, and the figure paused to gaze at us. I fought not to cry out. For a split second, I could have sworn The Bard of Avon was indeed standing there peering at me from dark hollow eye sockets.

"I can't be certain, but it sure looks like Shakespeare's ghost, doesn't it?" Charly asked. Domino growled and took a step forward. I couldn't tell if she was poised to pursue the apparition or merely taking a stance to protect us. The usually bold and sassy Emily cowered at Domino's side. Then the figure turned and appeared to vanish into the darkness.

"Robyn," I said suddenly overcome by the urgency to reach her. Before I could step off the curb, a new commotion approached. A golf cart, without the headlights on, came streaking toward us. The whine of the motor was barely discernible, but I heard raised voices. I was suddenly bathed in an eerie light as I struggled to see who or what was careening toward us.

"Faster, faster! We're losing him," a recognizable male voice exclaimed in a loud whisper.

"Over my dead body," the driver responded. Even though he'd been urged to speed up, he slowed for a moment as he passed us. "Excuse us if we don't stop! Don't worry, either, we'll have Shakespeare cornered in no time. We ain't afraid of no ghost!"

"Was that who I think it was?"

"As hard as it may be to believe, yes," Charly replied. We watched as they sped away toward the pedestrian bridge on the other side of the small park. The bridge allows residents of Seaview Cottages to go to the beach without having to cross the sometimes-busy public roadway below. The road is the main route along the coastal dunes and beaches used by locals and tourists alike. It's also the way to the high-end beachfront, Blue Haven Resort, that's south of our community. I saw another streak of white as the figure they were pursuing became visible once again. Not for long, though.

"If Shakespeare beats them to the bridge, it won't matter whether they're scared of him or not. He's bound to get away," I muttered as I stepped into the street. "What on earth were they wearing?"

"If I had to guess, I'd say they were wearing night vision goggles—Joe driving, Carl riding shotgun." Charly took off ahead of me as we cut across the street at an angle toward Robyn's cottage.

"What was the thing Carl was holding?"

"I'm not sure. I doubt it was a dematerializer like the one Dan Aykroyd had with him in the Ghostbusters movie the guys seem intent on playing out in real life." When we stepped onto the curb not more than a few yards from Robyn's white picket fence, it hit me.

"I think it was a fire extinguisher or a large spray gun of some kind. If it's a loaded sprayer, I hope they're not using insecticide or anything toxic. If they are, the ghost won't be the only one keeling over when they unload whatever's in it."

"Now that I hear what you're saying, it could have been a paintball gun! It won't stop you if you're already dead, but a fake ghost might be wearing more than white if they can get to him before he hits the footbridge." As she said that, we heard a screech of tires and then the crunch of metal.

"I didn't know a golf cart could go fast enough to burn rubber, did you?"

"I don't think it's the golf cart." I paused and looked over my shoulder as Charly was doing. The colored, blinking lights were unmistakable. Members of the local constabulary had arrived.

"If the guys are putting us on, it serves them right if they get carted off by the police."

"I don't believe they'd go to such elaborate means to play a joke in the middle of the night. Those guys are early risers like we are, and this is way past their bedtime. Call Robyn and tell her we're here, will you? I'd like to speak to her and look around before the police join us."

"At this hour, at least we won't have to deal with Deputy Devers." With my phone in one hand and Domino's leash in the other, I dialed the number on my cellphone for Robyn. Her phone rang half a dozen times. I ended the call and reentered the numbers just in case I'd made a mistake when I'd previously entered them. "She's not answering. I was afraid I couldn't get through to her in her closet." I fiddled with the latch on the gate in front of the Shakespeare Cottage until Charly stopped me.

"Call her again," Charly said as she held the gate open for Domino and me. I walked toward the front door growing more anxious when Robyn still didn't respond. Built in the same style as my home, the Shakespeare Cottage is more California Bungalow than cottage per se. A large columned porch ran along the front, although this one also wrapped around the sides of the large structure. In the clear light of day, it's a comfortable, inviting place, but right now, it was pitch dark, and my stomach fluttered at the possibility that danger lurked in the darkness.

I motioned for Charly to wait as I swept the porch with the beam from my flashlight. I could see the steps as Domino, and I worked our way, slowly from one step to the next. Charly and Emily were on our heels. When we reached the top step, Domino growled. I stopped and scanned the porch from one end to the other. Two things made the hair on the back of my neck stand up.

"It's open," I whispered to Charly. "That's blood, isn't it?"

"Is the phone still ringing?" Charly asked in a whisper.

"Yes, but she hasn't answered it," I said.

"Then let's go find her. Now!"

"Won't the police object if we don't wait for them?" I asked. To be honest, my expression of concern about violating police protocol was an attempt to buy a little time. A wave of nauseating cowardice had engulfed me. A bloody handprint on the doorframe and drops of blood on the porch had me paralyzed on the top step.

"She'll take cold comfort from our desire to be law-abiding citizens if she's in there injured, and we let her bleed to death."

"That can't be her blood we're looking at. The open door means any intruder has fled, don't you think?" The creepy vision of Shakespeare's ghost as he'd held us in his gaze gave me the shivers.

"That's about the best reason I can come up with for the front door to be wide open in the middle of the night. The handprint appears to be left by someone on the way out. Let's hope that means Robyn is still in her closet and too afraid to even answer her phone."

Charly picked up Emily and stepped in front of me as I held the flashlight on the open doorway. I followed, guiding Domino around a couple of blood drops as we entered the foyer. I searched the darkness with the beam from my flashlight.

"Give me another second, Charly. If there's more blood, I don't want us to step in it." I didn't want to break any laws or trash evidence that might be useful to the police. Dread had come back to haunt me. I hate the sight of blood—especially mine—but I'd prefer not to see anyone else's either.

"I don't see any more blood, do you?" Charly forced my hand to sweep the foyer and hallway again before responding to my anxious query.

"No. Whatever happened must have taken place as the intruder fled." Then another worry struck me.

"If Robyn is still hiding in her closet, scared out of her wits, how did the intruder get injured?"

"Good question. Robyn!" Charly called out.

I could hear the faint sound of Robyn's phone ringing from the back of the house where I knew her master bedroom was located. Domino whined as I took another step in the direction of the ringing. Then she woofed, and Emily followed suit.

"Robyn's got to be able to hear that." Before Charly could comment, I heard a groan. I ended the phone call, hoping I could figure out where the groaning had originated. Shuffling footsteps came from Robyn's study to our right. I raised my flashlight prepared to stop the fiend from getting any closer. As I did that, the beam of my flashlight caught a figure in the outer edges of the glow it cast.

"Don't hit me. I'm already sore all over."

"Neely?" I asked as I lowered my flashlight. Charly reached over and flipped on the lights in the foyer and then rushed to Neely's side. The dogs were delighted and almost knocked down Neely in their enthusiasm.

"What happened? Who did this?" Charly asked as she guided Neely to a chair in the den that opened to a spacious great room beyond. I searched that area as well as I could in the dim light cast by the overhead light in the foyer. When Neely was seated, Charly turned on a table lamp, dropped Emily's leash, and leaned over to examine Neely. Neely held her glasses in one hand and rubbed the back of her head with the other. I didn't see a wound anywhere, but there was blood on the shoulder of the gauzy, long-sleeved tunic she wore, and one sleeve was ripped at the shoulder seam.

"I'm not quite sure. Robyn called me in a state of absolute terror. She told me she was going to call you and Charly, but she thought I might still be up and could get here quicker. Shakespeare's ghost was cursing at someone, and she was afraid he was coming for her."

Distracted by Neely's story, I wasn't holding on to Domino's leash as tightly as I should have, and when Emily suddenly bolted toward the back of the house, Domino followed before I could tighten my grip. They were yipping and woofing, and their leashes made clanking sounds as they ran. I took a step toward the hallway and heard scratching at what I figured had to be the door to Robyn's master suite. They must have heard her moving about in there. I hit redial and called Robyn.

"Didn't she tell you any of this when she called you?" Neely asked as she examined her glasses. One of the hinges was loose, but she put them on anyway.

"Some of it, which is why we came running, too. She didn't say anything about anyone cursing or raise the possibility that there was a second intruder. You got here fast since your cottage isn't much closer than ours."

"Robyn was right that I was still up and dressed, so I took off. I got here faster than I ever dreamed I could. I'm in no condition for sprinting or wrestling, for that matter.

I let myself in with the spare key Robyn gave us after we did our walkthrough. It was completely dark, and before I could turn on a light, someone jumped out. I hadn't shut the front door, and some jerk shoved me from behind trying to get out. When I grabbed onto the sleeve of a windbreaker, I could tell it was a man."

"You grabbed him?" I gasped. Neely nodded.

"It was a desperate move. I wasn't trying to stop the dirt bag from getting away. I just didn't want to hit the floor, face first, at the rate of speed I was traveling. I've got plenty of padding, but not on my nose. When he couldn't shake me loose, he grabbed me by the shirt and yanked. That's when I heard my blouse rip. He pulled me close and tried to get me in a choke hold with his other arm. That's when I reared back and head-butted him." Neely rubbed her head again. "I must have made contact since I've got his blood on me. His nose wasn't any better padded than mine."

"Did he knock you out?" Charly asked.

"No, but I must have come close to knocking myself out because I don't remember much after head-butting him until I heard you call Robyn's name."

"Were there two intruders in the house like Robyn told you?" Neely frowned as she pondered Charly's question. Then her eyes widened.

"There had to be. Before the guy shoved me, I heard footsteps in the hallway. I'd taken a step inside from the porch into the foyer and had just turned toward the study when I stopped to see if someone was running down the hall. That's when the big galoot shoved me, and I held onto him for dear life." Charly made eye contact with me.

"I don't believe her attacker was Shakespeare's ghost, do you?"

"The guy's arm you grabbed wasn't glowing was it?" I asked Neely who stared at me and then at Charly in bewilderment before replying.

"No glow—just that funky windbreaker fabric in a dark color. I doubt it was a ghost running down the hallway either. Unless I've missed something, in the stories I've read, ghosts glide or float, dragging chains maybe. By the sound of the pounding on the hallway floor, the guy was no lightweight nor was he fleet of foot, so I'd say he wasn't a ghost either." She was about to make another comment when we all startled at the sound of a disembodied voice.

3

Windy Side of the Law

"Still you keep o' the windy side of the law: good."
—Twelfth Night

∞

"**M**IRIAM," THE VOICE called out plaintively. If I was being contacted from the other side by Shakespeare's ghost, he had a surprisingly high-pitched voice. When I heard the voice again, I snapped to, and pressed the phone to my ear!

"Robyn, it's me. I'm here. Neely and Charly are, too. You can come out now." I strode down the hallway, turning on lights as I went. When I reached the kitchen, I paused, puzzled to see that Domino and Emily were in there. The digging I'd heard continued. Not at the door to Robyn's bedroom, but the one to her walk-in pantry. I froze. Was someone hiding in there?

"What is it you guys?" I asked trying to sound nonchalant as I ambled toward them. "Are you hungry?" The dogs grunted but kept pawing at the door. I dashed to Robyn's kitchen table, grabbed one of the wooden chairs, and wedged it under the doorknob. Once I'd done that, the dogs stopped scratching, and watched me. They were as quiet as little mice as I leaned against the door and listened. I'm not sure what I expected to hear. Heavy breathing, maybe, if a beastly culprit was leaning in the same way against the other side of the door.

"What are you doing?" A voice bellowed not more than a few inches behind me. I shrieked, spun around, and struck out. A man's hand grabbed my arm at the last second, or Deputy Devers would have taken a blow to the side of his head from my flashlight. He blanched when he realized what had almost happened, then turned a deep red color as fear turned to anger. "How dare you! I have half a mind to arrest you for assaulting an officer of the law."

Half a mind sounded about right to me. I was tempted to yank my arm free and finish the job if I was going to go to jail anyway. So much for my earlier concerns about whether I'd be able to use the flashlight as a weapon. In less than five minutes, I'd nearly felled two people. I felt the grip on my arm tighten.

"No harm, no foul, Darnell. I'm not sure what all has gone on here, but I gather it's been a rough night." I nodded and heaved a huge sigh of relief. Hank Miller took the flashlight away from me before he let go of my arm.

"What are you doing here?" I asked. Detective Hank Miller is with the County Sheriff's Department. It had never occurred to me when I'd told Robyn to call 911 that the detective would respond to a call about a break-in.

"That ought to be my line, don't you think?" He asked with no twinkle in his eye. I tried not to smile at his exasperation. Even in the middle of the night, weary and annoyed, he was a fine-looking man I guessed to be in his fifties.

"We should stop meeting like this, if that's what you're driving at," I quipped. He hung his head, as if in despair, but the twinkle in his eyes was back.

"Rough night! That's an understatement," Robyn wailed interrupting our exchange. "Look at this disaster!"

I'd been so focused on keeping whoever was in the pantry locked up, and shocked by the unexpected encounter with our police pals that I'd hardly noticed the disarray in Robyn's usually tidy kitchen. A side table near the door to Robyn's garage was overturned. A lovely watercolor of sunflowers that had been hanging above it had fallen to the floor, scattering shards of glass around it. The backing had been pulled off, and the frame was bent. Coins, papers, and other items that must have been on the table were all over the floor, too. A clear liquid oozed from beneath the door to Robyn's pantry.

"Your friends in the study told us the door was open and the intruders had fled. Is somebody in there?" Deputy Devers asked in an annoyed tone.

"I didn't see or hear anyone, but the dogs were digging at the door, so I blocked the door. I didn't want to take a chance on an intruder getting away."

"Police!" Hank called out, pounding on the door. Domino whined, and Emily spun around as if we were all playing a new game. "If you've got a weapon, put it down and come out with your hands up."

"Get these dogs under control!" Devers demanded as Emily and Domino barked out orders of their own. As far as I could tell by their reactions, the closest thing to a bad guy anywhere near us was the cranky deputy. Emily bared her tiny teeth at the surly deputy. Charly, who'd been examining the kitchen, stepped closer, bent down, and scooped Emily up in her arms. I grabbed Domino's leash.

"Heel!" I commanded as I stepped back next to Charly several feet away from the pantry door.

"You shouldn't call him that to his face. Devers will have you hauled off to the hoosegow for disturbing his peace," Neely whispered as she joined us from where she'd been standing in the arched entryway leading into Robyn's kitchen.

"Sit!" I commanded, trying to suppress a nervous giggle in response to Neely's snide remark. Deputy Devers must not have heard her, but Hank did. He shook his head "no" at Neely.

"Let's see what we've got," the deputy said. He hoisted his pants up a tad, and then placed one hand on his holstered gun as he used the other to remove the chair from in front of the pantry door. Hank turned the doorknob, eased it open a crack, and waited. It was so quiet you could have heard a pin drop. Then, the detective slipped the toe of his shoe into the door opening and slung it wide. We gasped. No intruder came barreling out of there, but the pantry was a disgusting sight.

"Oh, no!" Robyn cried. "I told you someone was in my house. Do you believe me now?"

"Do you keep anything of value in there?" Hank asked.

"Do you mean something besides a few hundred dollars' worth of groceries? I'm a firm believer in disaster preparedness, and you're looking at several months of food on the floor—beans, rice, flour, cooking oil. Why would Shakespeare's ghost do such a thing?" Robyn asked. Devers shook his head.

"How bad is your cooking if they're sending messengers from the dead to stop you?" he asked, smirking.

"Hank's already told you to cool it, Devers." Charly spoke with such authority that the deputy's mouth popped open, but he shut it without uttering another word.

"What Hank is getting at, Robyn is that some people hide their mad money in a cookie jar or an ordinary-looking item, stashed in a place like a pantry. You don't have jewelry secreted in a fake baking powder can or a cereal box safe, or anything like that, do you?" Robyn appeared mystified by the question.

"I've never had much worth hiding. Why would it have occurred to me to do that? When I tried to convince you that someone had been in my cottage moving things around, I could have added that they were wasting their time if they were hoping I have valuables to steal. Of course, the ghost has never done anything this bad before, so maybe he's angry because I don't have anything worth stealing. I bet you won't call me a daffy old dame anymore, will you, Deputy?"

"Not if I can believe you didn't do this yourself."

"Why would I?"

"For the attention, maybe. Or as part of some scheme that you and your pals in the golf cart have cooked up. Wrapping themselves around a tree in the middle of the night while chasing ghosts ought to be a lesson learned. Not just any ghost either but Shakespeare's ghost, no less. How do you all come up with this bunk?"

"I can assure you, Devers, that even Shakespeare would agree we've all stayed on the 'windy side of the law' tonight." Devers cocked his head to one side.

"The windy side is the right side of the law, Darnell," Hank added, interpreting for the deputy. Then Hank addressed Charly. "You and your friends cut it close, staying on the windy side of the law by a hair's breadth. I can't say the same for the ghost patrol who are, at the very least, going to get ticketed."

"What's happened to Joe and Carl? Are they all right?" I asked.

"They're okay, but the golf cart has seen better days," Hank replied. "It appears they were driving without their headlights in pursuit of Shakespeare's ghost and didn't see the tree until it was too late. Driving without the use of their headlights is only one of their many misdeeds." If he'd intended to describe a litany of misdeeds, I cut him off.

"Where did he go?"

"Who? The ghost?" Hank asked. I wobbled my head not sure whether a yes or no was the correct answer.

"For want of a better understanding of what we witnessed tonight, ghost will do for now." Charly and I gave Hank and the deputy the best rendition of what we'd seen during our brief encounter with a glowing apparition bearing a remarkable resemblance to Shakespeare. Robyn gasped when she heard what we had to say.

"Where did Shakespeare go?" I asked again. "Did you send anyone after him?"

"No, we didn't. When we examined the pedestrian walkway, which your friends claim the ghost used as an exit route, there was no one around to pursue."

"I told you The Bard walks again!" Robyn wailed.

"It's more like he's running, at this point. Even before Joe and Carl were chasing him." Then, Neely filled them in on her misadventure that occurred before Charly and I arrived.

"I already told you there were two of them. I heard them quarreling! Maybe Shakespeare wasn't mad at me and two warring ghostly entities fought it out in my pantry." Robyn's remark was followed by a resounding silence before Neely picked up the conversation. I was grateful because I couldn't figure out how to respond to Robyn's warring entities remark.

"I never got a glimpse of the one running down the hall, but Charly and Miriam saw someone with the visage of Shakespeare coming from the direction of this cottage. That must be the ghostly figure Robyn saw before she hid in her bedroom and started calling people for help." She shrugged, rubbed her head again, and yawned, setting off a chain reaction. The evening was catching up with Neely, even though she was the veteran night owl among us. I had no doubt the figure Charly and I had seen was the same one that had sent Robyn into a panic. If for no other reason than improbability that there could be more than one phantom Shakespeare on the loose in Seaview Cottages.

"If anyone escaped from this end of the house, he must have used your sliders." Devers stepped toward the patio doors as if he was going to check to see if they were open. Hank reached out and stopped him.

"Let's wait for the crime lab investigators to dust for

prints, Darnell. Do you have someplace you can stay tonight, Robyn?"

"With me," we all replied at once. Robyn smiled for the first time since she'd joined us.

"I'll stay with Neely. That way I can make sure she's really okay after busting that guy's nose with the back of her head." Neely, Charly, and I all nodded. Having someone to check on her was a good idea since Neely had refused to go to the ER and get X-rays. She was lucky to end up with nothing worse than a bump on the head and a few aches and pains. So was the intruder if he got away from her with only a broken nose or a fat lip given her resourcefulness. He was even more fortunate not to have encountered Charly with her kubotan or me with my apparently wanton willingness to lay waste to suspected ne'er-do-wells with the flashlight of doom.

"You know what? If Neely's attacker exited via the front door, while Shakespeare's ghost went out the back, they must have left at about the same time. Unless the guy in the windbreaker took a different escape route out on the street, he would have crossed our path just as his ghostly companion did."

"Good point! Maybe Carl and Joe spotted a person in a dark-colored windbreaker," Neely suggested. "They were driving toward the Shakespeare Cottage from the opposite end of the street when they spoke to Charly and Miriam, although I have no idea why they were out after midnight."

"Neighborhood ghost patrol," Hank muttered. "They told us they didn't see anyone until they spotted Shake-speare right before they nearly bumped into you two in the literal sense of the word. Even if someone had been on the street, I doubt they would have seen a figure in dark clothes while driving with their headlights off."

"Or maybe he vanished into thin air by then, too. Mercy me, all I need is two ghosts! Nasty, quarreling foul-mouthed ghosts. Immortal enemies maybe, but far from what I'd call ghostly companions, Miriam."

"Point taken," Charly noted. "One thing's for certain, though, Robyn. Ghosts don't bleed. At least one of your unwelcome visitors does." The grim tone in Charly's voice chilled me to the bone.

4

Wild Goose Chase

"Nay, if our wits run the wild-goose chase, I am done."

—Romeo & Juliet

∞

"WE ALMOST HAD him! If we hadn't hit that tree as hard as we did, we could have gone after him on foot."

"How long did you expect your wild goose chase to last?" Midge asked. "You two would have been lucky to make it to the other side of the bridge before you collapsed, especially if you were hauling that paintball gun and the tank with you."

"Midge is right. She was a nurse for a long time and has seen plenty of much younger people, including healthy Army recruits, overdo it. You ought to be grateful you hit that tree, or we might be at your bedside in a hospital—or worse." Marty had that right. In fact, we were all fortunate no one ended up in the hospital with two intruders wreaking havoc at the Shakespeare Cottage.

"What were you going to do with a paintball gun if

you did catch up with Shakespeare's ghost?" I asked. Joe sat up abruptly and banged the coffee table in front of him with his knee. We all grabbed our drinks afraid they'd spill on the gleaming wood table or fluffy white Sherpa carpet beneath it.

Marty, who'd worked for decades as a buyer for high-end department stores, had decorated her Fitzgerald Cottage with beautiful, expensive items. The place was a showcase with hints of art deco design that screamed Gatsby as if readied for a magazine photo shoot. I couldn't imagine her kitchen covered in flour and crumbs like mine often ends up after a baking binge.

I've never made as big a mess as the one in Robyn's kitchen. We'd asked her to join us for dinner, but she'd gone home late this afternoon to clean up. At least she wasn't facing the cleanup alone. Her landlord, who'd been dismissive about previous complaints of intruders, had hired help.

"Relax, you guys. I'm not living in a museum. Cats are amazingly agile, but Scheherazade knocks stuff over all the time. She can be a bad cat when she wants to be." Marty laughed as if she was joking, but I could believe it. Domino and Emily were home alone tonight because Scheherazade doesn't tolerate the presence of dogs. "Believe it or not, sometimes she even pushes my things off onto the floor on purpose."

I could believe that, too. Scheherazade was watching us from where she lounged on the back of Marty's chair. When Marty spoke her name, her enormous fluffy white tail switched, batting Marty in the face. I'm normally as big a fan of cats as I am of dogs, but this one made me uneasy. When I'd arrived, her golden eyes had lingered disapprovingly on me, perhaps sniffing eau du Domino on my clothing. By the way she'd glared at Joe when he banged the table, I suspect she may not like people any better than dogs. Not even her owner all the time given what Marty said about the mischief the enormous Persian cat caused.

"Since you didn't answer Miriam, I'll ask the question again in a slightly different way. What were you going to do if you'd cornered the ghost?" Marty asked getting us back on topic.

"We thought if we hit him with a paintball and the paint stuck, we'd have proof he's no ghost," Carl replied.

"It also might have been enough to slow him down so we could grab him and sit on him until security or the police got there. The neighborhood ghost patrol would have made its first citizens' arrest."

"Someone needs to stop the rat from impersonating one of the greatest writers of all time. Who does he think he is?" Midge huffed in a gruff ex-Army nurse way. I'm not sure why, but her outrage caught me by surprise.

"I had no idea you were a fan of Shakespeare." I still have so much to learn about my interesting new friends at Seaview Cottages. True friends who'd forgiven the little white lies I'd told. They'd helped me come up with a solution to the problems I faced as an underage resident in the fifty-five plus community.

"It's no secret I'm something of an Anglophile which is obvious since I live in the Jane Austen Cottage. I toyed with the idea of taking to the stage before I found my calling as a nurse. Not to mention, I have an ordinary face, and I'm built like a tank. In the theater that's not *the stuff as dreams are made on*, to steal a line from The Bard. Who wouldn't be a fan of a person who said it all so eloquently hundreds of years ago?" Midge paused, and her entire demeanor changed to one I'd never seen before. Her voice changed, too as she spoke.

> *"All the world's a stage,*
> *And all the men and women merely players;*
> *They have their exits and their entrances,*
> *And one man in his time plays many parts."*

It was as if she'd been transported and we were taken with her as she uttered those words with an ethereal quality in her tone. Then she snapped to—back into the no-nonsense, tough-as-nails nurse. Her flight of poetic fancy stood in stark contrast to her usual persona. The woman had spent a big chunk of her life in a profession that required stringent adherence to reason, logic, and rules vital to saving lives. I understand that part of her character very well since bookkeepers live by rules, too.

"Women too, of course, not just men, play many parts. The soliloquy goes on to describe the seven stages in life. There's so much in these few phrases, though. Have you ever heard a truer or more succinct commentary on our existence?"

"Well, I don't speak Shakespeare—all the 'tis, thou, whilst, and doth loses me every time."

"There wasn't a bit of that in what Midge just shared with us," Charly snapped. "Besides, we all speak Shakespeare almost every day without even realizing it. When Midge asked you about the wild goose chase you were on, it obviously wasn't the first time you've heard those words. You've probably used them many times, too. The phrase comes from a line in Romeo and Juliet." Neely jumped in eagerly.

"You know how much I love Agatha Christie's Miss Marple, Conan Doyle's Sherlock Holmes, and so many other wonderful mystery writers and their characters. 'The game is afoot' is a line that first came from Shakespeare's pen, not from one of my favorite mystery authors." Neely was understating her devotion to stories of murder and mayhem in books and in movies. Every nook and cranny of her Christie Cottage is crammed with memorabilia and books, including some early editions that are valuable and probably ought to be behind lock and key. Shakespeare's ghost would have made out like a bandit if he'd chosen to break in at Neely's place, or here at Marty's cottage. Which made me wonder aloud about the location of the latest incident.

"Why break into the Shakespeare Cottage?"

"By the destruction in the pantry, it's obvious some-one's looking for something. I also believe Robyn's claims that she's had uninvited guests on earlier occasions who searched other areas of the cottage. That's not the behavior of opportunistic thieves going house-to-house to pilfer silverware or jewelry."

"Assuming they're not on a wild goose chase, what could they be searching for?"

"That's what she's hired G.O.L.D. to discover," Charley replied. "I'll get a copy of the police report and the crime lab results, too, as soon as they're available. Maybe they'll contain some hint of who was in there or what they were after." Charly was the only one of us who had the connections to get that kind of information and who could do it quickly.

"Whatever someone's looking for can't be too big if it could have been hidden in a tin of baking powder or a bag of flour," Midge observed.

"That's probably true. The crime lab investigators will do their best to sift through the debris for fingerprints and other clues about the identity of the intruders. They took Neely's blouse and collected samples of the blood left at the scene. If they can determine who's been in there, maybe Hank can haul them in for questioning and ask why."

"It's probably way too late to get DNA from Shakespeare unless they can dig up his old bones. Do ghosts leave DNA?"

"Stop it, Joe. The ghostbusters thing isn't funny anymore," Midge said.

"You didn't see what we saw," Carl added. "Besides, there's more than one way to bust a ghost. I told you we were out to get the guy—dead or alive!"

"We did see him," Charly responded. "From a distance, it sure looked like Shakespeare's ghost—glowing one minute and gone the next. How much of that could have been done with makeup, Neely?"

"A wig and a period costume wouldn't be hard to find. As for the glow, you could add that to the skin using body paint or to the costume by mixing glow paint into fabric paint. If you expose phosphorescent paint to sunlight, it'll glow for hours."

"What about the vanishing act?" I asked.

"A cloak of invisibility," Joe replied. "I mean, that's if we're not dealing with a real ghost that's capable of materializing and dematerializing at will." I paused, not sure if he was clowning around again or still seriously considering the prospect that we were dealing with a ghost. Neely looked at Joe and then at me.

"I'm sure Joe's trying to be funny—sort of—but the cloak of invisibility angle isn't completely dumb. A dark cloak thrown over the costumed figure might make him appear to vanish. That might explain how he seemingly disappeared right in front of Robyn, too. It's too bad she didn't just turn on the overhead light in the hallway. That would have exposed his charade for what it was."

"We can ask Robyn about that, although I believe she tried that the first time he appeared, and the light didn't come on."

"Spooky, huh?" Joe asked adding a few ghost hoots. "When that first incident occurred, she called 911, but by the time the police arrived, there was no sign of anyone in her cottage. No evidence of a break-in and the light in the hallway worked fine, too."

"Monkeying with a circuit breaker is no big deal if someone was out to give Robyn a good scare," Carl suggested. "It worked, too, since she pretty much just ran for it after that—especially once Devers called her the next day and ran his daffy dame number on her."

"The elaborate Shakespeare's ghost getup took some doing and worked well to keep Robyn from reporting an intruder or being believed when she did. Why have your partner drop in wearing a plain old warmup suit or whatever it was the assailant you head-butted had on, Neely?"

"They didn't act like partners, and Shakespeare's ghost was always alone on his previous visits."

"So, partners or not, this visit was different. When she'd seen him before, it was always in the hallway and not in the kitchen where there was such a mess this time. The police report ought to tell us if the sliders were open and the intruder got out that way. Maybe one or both got *in* that way too." Charly sipped her drink. "To me, the sliders in the kitchen appeared to be locked. I'm not expecting them to find anything."

"What about the door leading from the garage to the back yard?" I asked.

"Let's see what Hank says. I'll also ask for the report filed the first time Robyn called 911. I doubt they reported anything suspicious or Devers wouldn't have called her in such a snit."

"What if there's an extra set of keys floating around? They could have come in the same way you did, Neely, without it looking like a break-in last night or in the past. Although, I'm not sure I understand where your attacker came from or why he didn't run for it down the hallway, too."

"It was pitch black in there, and my eyes aren't so great anyway. I was still adjusting to the change from the brighter light outdoors near the streetlamps. He was wearing dark clothes, so maybe he was standing right in front of me. My eyesight is so poor, I might not have noticed him until he moved."

"I'd say hiding behind the door is more like it," Joe offered. "Robyn may not have seen the ghost in the kitchen, but she's noticed that things were moved around in the study and other parts of the house."

"That includes the master suite, too," Midge pointed out. "Shakespeare didn't always sneak around in the middle of the night, either. Sometimes, after Robyn returned home from an outing or errand, she noticed items in the cottage had been rearranged."

"Do we have specific dates to go with the earlier incidents when she noticed items had been moved?"

"I don't know, Charly," Joe replied. "Do you, Carl?"

"No, but putting together a timeline is a great idea. Someone should ask her about dates once she's had a chance to calm down and can think straight. She first called her landlord worried that someone had been in the cottage not long after she renewed her lease almost a year ago. That's when he brought up the possibility that it was a ghost. Robyn took him seriously, but I don't know the guy, so maybe he was kidding."

"Let's ask him," I suggested. "Are we sure the landlord hasn't been snooping around in her cottage? He'd have the keys."

"He'd also have permission, with some advance notice, to inspect the premises, so no snooping required. If she renewed her lease, that must mean she was living there almost a year before trouble started," Midge observed.

"Or before she noticed it," Marty added. "It's easy to dismiss stuff at our age. I hide things from myself on occasion. Especially the first few months when she was moving in, it might not have occurred to her that an item wasn't where she expected to find it."

"Talking to the landlord and getting his view on what's occurred should be straightforward now that he can't deny something's going on in the Shakespeare Cottage," Charly said.

"I hope you're right. Joe and I weren't out last night on a lark, no matter how it may seem. We need to figure this out sooner rather than later because last night's incident wasn't just different; it was more desperate and deranged. Is Robyn going to be safe returning to the cottage?" Carl asked. That question landed in the room like a lead balloon.

5

What's in a Name?

"What's in a name? That which we call a rose by any other name would smell as sweet."
—Romeo and Juliet

∞

"ROBYN'S STAYING WITH me tonight. We weren't sure that the cleanup would get done today. All the locks are being changed on her doors, and the code's being reset on the alarm system, so they'll make the place as secure as anyone can."

"Even if they get the pantry, foyer, and porch cleaned, there must be touch-ups and repainting that need to be done. That's going to stink the place up. Keep her out of there for a few days—at night, anyway." Joe was so adamant that I knew he was up to something.

"Are you hoping if Robyn leaves the cottage empty, the ghost will return?" I asked.

"It could happen. Why not give the old guy room to roam if that's what he wants to do?"

"You too, Carl? I thought you understood you'd wiggled out of legal trouble by agreeing to give up your ghost patrol." Midge sounded gruff, but I could tell she didn't completely disapprove.

"That's true. We said no more ghost patrol, but no one said anything about no stakeouts," Carl replied.

"You're more likely to stay out of trouble if we set up surveillance cameras and spy on the cottage—inside and out that way. If Robyn will agree to stay out of there, we won't violate her privacy."

"I can do that," Joe said. "One nanny cam, coming up!"

"If we leave, now, we'll have time to go to more than one store to find what we need. Robyn will have to let us in, but I can have the inside camera installed in no time at all." Carl leaned forward as if he was ready to leave.

"You should set up several of them," Charly said with growing enthusiasm. "How about one in the foyer, if you can find a place to hide it? Our not too friendly ghost appears to like to hang out in the hallway, so a good view of the hallway would be great. You should also set up a second one in the kitchen, and a third one in the den or the great room."

"How about the master suite?" I asked. "She's hardly ever been out of there. If the ghost returns and finds the house empty and the door to her suite wide open, maybe that'll entice him into that room. You could set up a camera on her dresser with a direct view of anyone entering through the doorway."

"This all assumes Shakespeare didn't find what he was looking for in the pantry." Marty was deep in thought. "It can't hurt, though, can it? Do you need me to kick in on the cost? I've never bought them, but they can't be cheap."

"Hey, I'm rolling in it now that Edgar paid all our annual assessments for us—for next year, too!" That had been a wonderful surprise. That news, in addition to the decision by the HOA's Executive Committee to approve the eighty/twenty provision allowing some Seaview Cottages residents to be younger than fifty-five, had given me a new lease on life.

"In a way, that's our first fee for sleuthing, so I'm happy to contribute to the costs, too. We also have the small retainer Robyn insisted on paying. I don't want security to pick you up for loitering after dark, but you also need to come up with a spot to mount a camera outside."

"I know those guys. We'll stay out of trouble by getting security to help us. How about that?"

"If they're willing to do it, why not? They might like the idea of having a camera that also covers the gate leading onto the footbridge since this isn't the first time a nonresident has used the bridge in a way the developers never intended."

"You haven't had dessert yet," I said. "Let's eat and then you can go."

"Hold on. I want to show you something, and then we can eat," Neely responded. "If Robyn's up for it, and we can both keep our eyes open, I'll get her to work on the timeline. She might even find it interesting to help us organize events in that way. I don't mind if she stays with me until we get a better handle on what's going on."

"That's great if she'll agree to do it. I don't believe Robyn's a target or knows anything that will help our increasingly impatient thief find what he, and last night's new burglar, want to find." Charly yawned. "I guess, technically, it was this morning not last night, wasn't it?"

"You're right about that. We ought to keep this short tonight, hoping we can all get home and catch up on our sleep. I'm sure you're also right that Robyn's in trouble just because she's in the wrong place. The ghost has done his best to scare her out of there, but what if Shakespeare misunderstands her unwillingness to leave?" A little ripple of uneasiness swept around the room.

"It is odd, isn't it? If I were her, especially after the latest fiasco, I'd be asking to get out of my lease. Does her landlord manage any other properties in the community?"

"That's a good question. Since I know him, I can talk to the landlord if you think it's appropriate. He may have been joking when he told Robyn it might be a ghost, but I'll bet there's more to it than that. He manages lots of properties, and I don't believe he'd enter a tenant's cottage without permission. I could have it all wrong..." We all eyed Marty wondering what to make of the hesitation in her voice.

"Stop with the penetrating gazes. I should have realized I'd get you snoops going. Robyn's landlord and I dated for a while, and I don't want to mix business and personal matters if you consider it a bad idea. Should I call George Pierson or not?" Scheherazade did not hesitate to make her opinion known. At the mention of George Pierson's name, she hissed and then took off. "Oh, Princess, please don't go. I won't bring him home, I promise."

Too late! The princess stopped, looked over her shoulder, and meowed. She grumbled as she flounced away with her big tail switching.

"As you can probably tell, they didn't get along. I'm sure he won't mind talking to us about the situation at Robyn's cottage. I just don't want to give him any reason to believe I'm trying to rekindle our relationship."

"If it would be less awkward for you, I'd be happy to go with you to have lunch with him at the club. Or if you don't want to stir up gossip by being seen with him, even with me along as a chaperone, we could have lunch at my house," I offered.

"I'm not worried about gossip, but if we meet at your cottage, he's more likely to see it as a visit you initiated than me. When?"

"Tomorrow, if that works for him, or the next day. He doesn't have a problem with dogs, does he?"

"No. He owns the cutest little cocker spaniel—or he did. It's been more than a year since we dated. I've run into him a couple of times in Duneville Downs, but never with Cookie. I hope that doesn't mean she's gone to the Rainbow Bridge."

"I won't bring it up unless he does. At least, he won't be uncomfortable with Domino."

"She won't mind, either. Domino likes everybody," Joe said. Then he shut up.

"Princess is picky and so am I. George is a nice-looking man, polite, well-traveled, and still working as a property manager even though he's a retired mining engineer. A little too obsessed with dirt and rocks for my taste." We were staring at her again. "What? I'm sure he was good at his job; I'm just not interested in how you know what dirt tells you about where to dig for oil or sink a shaft to mine for ore. I tried. I even went to one of those rock shows with him. Not my thing, I'm afraid. I don't want to understand dirt. I just need to keep it out of my house!"

"Let's see what he has to say about where that ghost story came from if he didn't just make it up to get Robyn to back off."

"Oh, he didn't make it up. George mentioned the haunting of Shakespeare Cottage to me in passing, but not in any detail and I didn't ask. All I recall is that the man who inherited the property prefers to live in Santa Barbara, and his wife insists the cottage is haunted. I'm not sure if she ever claimed it was Shakespeare prowling around." Marty shrugged.

"Let's ask him. We'll also see if he'll give us information about how to contact the owners. I'd love to hear what the wife has to say. Her encounters with a ghost would have occurred long before Robyn's did."

"I'm a mining engineer of sorts, too! Cyber mining is a compulsion of mine when it comes to unsolved mysteries. I started digging into the background on the story of Shakespeare's Cottage, and I've already struck pay dirt." That got our attention.

"Shakespeare Cottage was one of the first residences built in Seaview Cottages. It was built by members of a family that owned all the acreage on which our community was eventually built. Apparently, when the property was sold back in the late 1950s, special provisions were made for the sellers to continue to live on the property in their old house. That's still the biggest lot in here. The original home was a much larger structure and wasn't torn down until Seaview Cottages went into development in the sixties." Neely pulled out a sheet of paper and handed it to

Charly who was sitting next to her. "Here's what I wanted to show you."

"Oh my, that is gorgeously creepy," Charly commented as she passed the photo on. "It's like a larger version of Norman Bate's house in *Psycho*."

"Or a set for one of those old Hammer Studios Gothic horror pictures starring Christopher Lee," Carl added, holding the photo so Joe could see it too.

"*I only vant to suck your blood*," Joe clowned in a ridiculous accent, throwing his head back, and curling his upper lip to expose his front teeth.

"Dracula never said that, but if you were trying to creep me out, you succeeded." Neely's mane of silver-tinged curls bounced wildly as she shook her head vigorously in response to his antics.

"Then my work here is done." Joe stood, bowed, and sat down again. "Maybe we should diversify, Carl, and become the first members of the neighborhood ghost and vampire patrol."

"Charly's Angels, at your service—on the lookout for all things undead. How about that?"

"How about you both stop it? I don't need to be creeped out more than I already am. No wonder they tore down that deathtrap and built a cottage on the spot instead." Marty quickly passed the photo to Midge.

"Make that health hazard and death trap," Midge added. "Did someone live in it until it was demolished?"

"It looks rundown, doesn't it? So far, there's no record that it was condemned before they tore it down. So, someone could have lived there."

"Deathtrap is right," I said when I took the photo

from Midge. Gazing at the large ornate residence with a rickety-looking verticality gave me vertigo. Unlike the *Psycho* house, though, it sat amid overgrown gardens not atop a hill. "The first question that pops into my mind looking at the headless statue lying on the ground isn't did someone live in it, but did someone die in it?"

"Funny you should ask. As it happens, there were several deaths at Hempstead Towers long before it was in such poor condition."

"Thanks, Miriam and Neely, now I've got goosebumps!" Marty rubbed her arms.

"Was it *murrrder* most foul?" Joe asked, back to speaking in his lousy attempt at a Dracula voice, I think.

"That's not clear."

"Who died?" Midge asked.

"The house was built at the turn of the century in the Victorian Gothic style. I haven't had time to track down much background on the original occupant, Stanley R. Hempstead, but it was built during one of those periods when there was lots of buzz about the railroad turning this area into the 'Atlantic City of the West Coast.' My guess is I might find his name if I dig deeper into the identities of the entrepreneurs with those ambitions. The first reported death occurred not long after the house was built when poor Stanley 'shuffled off this mortal coil,' to steal a few more choice words from Shakespeare."

"How did he die?" I asked Neely.

"The short account I've found refers to his death as a tragic accident, and there aren't many details. Built in 1906, the house was one of the first private residences to be wired for electricity. Apparently, something went wrong, and Stanley Hempstead was electrocuted. That set off a round of hoopla in the news—not just local news, but in LA and San Francisco. There was huge opposition to the use of electricity, and his death fueled the fury. Maybe someone rigged it to fail, or he did himself in. Who knows for sure? I'm not certain there was a formal investigation into his death."

"Coroners are still hesitant to rule a death a suicide—even if there's a formal inquest. I'll see if I can get anything from the police archives if there are records of the incident. You're right that there may not have been an investigation depending on how Mr. Hempstead's family handled his death. Families have always been inclined to keep authorities from intruding into personal matters like suicide. That's often true about a homicide, too, if he was a victim of foul play that involved family members."

"Stanley Hempstead was the first to die, but he wasn't the last. Stanley's son died in a drowning accident around the anniversary of his father's death. A year later, a young man who was tending the formal gardens created to give the large home a stately presence, was killed when he fell from a ladder. There's no reference to ghosts yet, but as you can see in this headline, the deaths earned the place a reputation as cursed."

Hempstead Towers Curse Strikes Again!

"The property was bought soon after the third death by an early ancestor of the De Voss family who eventually sold it to the Seaview Cottages developers. As soon as they bought it, they changed the name to Seaview Bluffs Manor."

"As if that mattered," Midge scoffed. "What's in a name? We didn't need Shakespeare to tell us that a rose by any other name smells as sweet. Surely the same can be said for a place that's cursed."

"I hope not! We all live here now!" Marty wailed.

"I don't believe in curses or ghosts. Did the deaths stop?" I asked.

"For a decade or so. In the 1920s, trouble erupted again at Seaview Bluffs Manor. I don't believe in curses or ghosts, either," Neely asserted. "I've just started delving into their past, and I've already come across a few interesting tidbits to suggest that the descendants of Rupert and Hilda De Voss, who bought the property from the Hempstead family, have a few skeletons in their closets."

6

The Game is Afoot

"Before the game is afoot, thou still let'st slip."
—**King Henry IV Part I**

∞

"**Y**OU DON'T MEAN actual skeletons, do you? In a large house like that, there must have been plenty of nooks and crannies in which to hide moldy old bones," Marty said. "Wouldn't the developers have found them when they tore it down?"

"I'm speaking metaphorically," Neely said. "Skeletons of the kind to which you're referring would have been found and laid to rest when they razed the structure in the early sixties. I've never heard that they found any, but maybe you can poke around in the community archives, Miriam, and see if anything like that happened."

"If someone found old bones among debris from a demolition today, the authorities would be called in. I'm not sure that would have been true fifty years ago. Besides, there's no reason to believe they had to hide bodies in the house when the family owned hundreds of acres of land," Midge pointed out.

"Now I'm curious. I'll do as you suggested, Neely, and see what I can find in the historical section of the community records. I'm not sure if all that information is online. What sort of skeletons are you talking about?"

"Give me another day to continue my mining activities before I give you all the details. Why don't you ask Robyn's landlord about ghosts and skeletons when you quiz him? Ask him about the curse, too, and whether he's heard rumors that members of the De Voss family were mixed up with bootlegging or other illicit activities."

"Here's another question to ask while you're at it," Carl suggested. "If the owners aren't interested in living in the cottage, why haven't they sold it? It's tough to make money on a rental property."

"I've never had much interest in real estate, so I'm ignorant about what it takes to make money as a landlord. One day when George was griping that the owners were bugging him about an issue with the cottage, I asked why they didn't just sell it. He said there was some clause in the Will when the husband inherited the property that prevents him from doing it. Can that be true?" Marty asked.

"Maybe. When we meet him for lunch, let's see if he can tell us more about what he meant by that. It's also possible they haven't been interested in selling the cottage because prices were so depressed for years. Or they might eke out a profit if they own the property outright and don't have a mortgage. The Shakespeare Cottage is also exempt from the homeowner's association fees."

"It is?" Neely asked. "Why?"

"The exemption was written into the contract when

the land was purchased by the developers. I can find out more if you think it's relevant." I'm not sure why I made that statement because I was going to go have another look at the HOA files whether they thought it was relevant or not.

"Why not if it's not that hard to do? Are they exempt from the Special Assessments, too?" Charly asked.

"Yes."

"Okay, well, that's interesting," Carl commented. "I doubt any of this means the Shakespeare Cottage is a cash cow, but it may not be a money pit, either."

"Greta has stepped back from her role as the community realtor now that she's up to her neck in legal troubles. Whoever has taken over for her must have been given a little background about why a property on a premium lot can't be sold. I'll check with the new realtor tomorrow," Midge offered. "Right now, I want to try the dessert you brought us."

"What is it?" Neely asked.

"Strawberry Sheet Cake. Robyn loves strawberries. I baked it for her, hoping she'd be able to join us."

"Can we take ours to go?" Joe asked, standing up so quickly that he banged the table again. We all scanned the room looking for Scheherazade. Satisfied he wasn't going to be accosted by an angry cat, Joe continued. "I want to get to the store, buy the cameras, and set up the surveillance. If we can't figure out how to mount the outside camera, I'm going to use my clout with the security guys to get them to watch the cottage tonight."

"What clout?" Neely and Charly asked almost simultaneously.

"Don't underestimate Joe," Carl said shaking a finger at them. "He's a mechanical genius. There's not a vehicle on this property he can't fix. Members of the security crew not only drop by when the community-owned cars give them grief but in minutes, Joe can figure out what's wrong with their personal vehicles. That's a brainstorm, Joe. I'm getting too old for all night stakeouts." Joe beamed at all the praise.

So much for cake to-go, though. As soon as I'd cut pieces of cake for them, they practically inhaled them and then left. We sat back down in the great room to eat and summarize our efforts before going home. My fifty-year-old body and mind were running on empty, but, apparently, Neely's wasn't even though she's more than a decade older than me.

"Okay, so the game is afoot—what game is it?" Neely asked.

"If we were in the middle of one of your beloved Alfred Hitchcock psychological thrillers, Neely, I'd say someone has it in for Robyn and is trying to drive her mad."

"That's interesting, Marty," Charly commented. "The motive for a game like that is usually money or revenge. She told us she has no money, what about men?"

"She's never told me much about her love life, so I pried into it a little this morning before she left to supervise the cleanup. I asked her if there's an ex-husband or an old flame who could have broken into her cottage for some reason. Maybe to take back an engagement ring that has sentimental value even if it's not worth much money. Robyn scoffed at the idea. For good reason, too, since she's never been married. In fact, she claims she never had another serious relationship with anyone after her fiancé was killed in Vietnam in the early seventies."

"How sad is that?" I asked as Neely paused to eat a big mouthful of the dense pink cake on her plate. The rich icing is chock full of strawberries which gives it a delicious flavor to go with the cheery pink color.

"What's sad is that she's not eating this cake. I'm already getting a sugar buzz after two bites." As Marty said that, Scheherazade appeared out of nowhere and levitated onto the arm of the club chair in which Marty sat. She reached out and pawed at Marty's arm trying to move it toward her so she could get a bite of cake. Maybe she was enticed by the butter and cream in the icing.

"No, Princess, this is Mama's. All Mama's." Marty pulled a tiny treat from a pocket and gave it to Scheherazade who took it. The cat made little throaty sounds that sounded like grumbling to me. Marty must have thought so, too.

"She can gripe all she wants. Even I have my limits. Strawberry cake isn't cat food." Marty scarfed down another bite before speaking again. "What Robyn has told me about her past is that she lived a very boring, quiet life in Fresno as a librarian. She always dreamed of being able to walk along the beach every day. The location, plus the appeal to a former librarian of living in the Writers' Circle, made Seaview Cottages the perfect choice. She may not have money, but she'll come into some once she sells her condo in Fresno. When Robyn moved here, she put her condo up for rent instead of selling it. That way she could move back to Fresno if she didn't like it here."

"That's what she told me, too," Midge added. "Her condo is on the market, now. Has she ever said anything to any of you about a family member who might have a grudge because Robyn inherited grandma's china or a vintage brooch, or something seemingly petty like that?"

"I know she has a married sister in Fresno who's a widow. Maybe Rose has kids with an ax to grind against Aunt Robyn, but I've never heard anything about a troubled niece or nephew. If her sister has children and they're anything like their mother and aunt, it would be hard to imagine them turning out to be monsters that would break into Aunt Robyn's house and terrorize her. Rose is an oncology nurse with hospice care, and Robyn volunteered with her sister's organization. They're a couple of strong, caring, independent women, as far as I can tell, but what do I know?" Marty asked.

"Robyn comes across as a sweet, self-effacing woman who doesn't enjoy talking about herself. It's also possible that she's said so little about her past because there is a skeleton or two in her closet, too," Neely suggested with a tone of reluctance in her voice. "Robyn's never experienced anything like this latest incident. The ghostly intruder has been stealthy during his previous visits."

"The Shakespeare's ghost ruse is an elaborate one to employ by a niece or nephew out to reclaim a family heirloom. The scary ghost routine makes more sense if someone is searching for something in the cottage and is trying to conceal his identity or would prefer to search an empty cottage. Especially if the ghost is now moving on from stealth snooping to demolition. I don't have your experience dealing with criminal minds, Charly, so I'm in the 'what do I know' camp alongside Marty."

I thought about Pete's smiling face, and it triggered that wave of uncertainty about my ability to judge people. My husband's sudden death had left me with a financial mess to untangle rooted in a series of surprisingly bad decisions he'd made without revealing them to me. The man I'd married had been keeping secrets from me for years, including taking out a second mortgage on our house in Ohio. I'm not sure those secrets could be characterized as skeletons in a closet, but now that the shock of his death has worn off, I find the revelations disturbing.

"Would it be wrong to run a background check on our client?" We all glanced at Charly waiting to hear her response to Marty's question.

"I'll bet we won't need to do that. We're not the only ones trying to understand why someone has been in her cottage. Robyn isn't Hank's friend or neighbor, nor is she a client, so I'd be surprised if he didn't run a background check on her today. If she has a history of legal or money problems, he'll find it."

"What were he and Darnell doing there last night? My head hurt too bad to stick around and interrogate him. I heard you ask him, Miriam. Confess! What did the attractive detective who finds you so amusing tell you?"

"Don't look at me like that," I said blushing. "I'm still Mrs. Webster as far as he knows, and I'm not sure I like being a source of amusement to him. He didn't explain why he and the irksome deputy were out after midnight and responding to a call about a prowler. If anyone knows more about Hank Miller's agenda, it's Charly." All eyes were on Charly again. If she'd intended to keep it to herself, she yielded to the pressure and let out a big sigh as she responded.

"They're working a different case. I'm not privy to all the details, but it has something to do with smuggling counterfeit goods. I'm almost certain it's an offshoot of the investigation into one of Diana Durand's little sidelines. That probably explains why both Hank and Darnell are involved. If the smugglers are bringing in goods along the coast near here, my guess is that they were on a stakeout not far from here and responded to the call about a prowler thinking it might have something to do with their investigation."

"Hank may not tell us what's going on, but Darnell will. If I run a scenario like that by him as if I already know what's up, he'll bluster and accuse me of eavesdropping. Then, we'll know you're on the right track."

"That won't be necessary, Midge," Charly argued. "I've already been assured that I'm on the right track. As I said, I don't have the details, but I understand they have a body on their hands. A drowned man washed up on the rocks near Woolf Point. From the police report, it appears if he hadn't drowned, he probably would have died from a fractured skull. Even though there's no indication in that report about a tie-in to the smuggling investigation, it was brought to my attention as a reason for us to be careful with our snooping."

"All we need is to get mixed up in someone else's game," I said.

"The members of the smuggling ring are ruthless. Devers found one of the locals, who transported goods for them, dead in the trunk of an abandoned vehicle on the highway. That was the same day we found Diana's body."

"Oh, no!" Marty exclaimed. "No more dead bodies!"

"We'll be fine if we stay focused on Robyn, the cottage, the cottage's owners and tenants—current and past. Before they left, I reminded Joe and Carl that they're already in enough trouble with the authorities. So, surveillance cameras, yes. More night patrols, no. If they hadn't hit that tree, they would have chased Shakespeare's ghost down to the beach. Given how close we are to a number of spots with excellent anchorage and easy access to the beach from the water, they could have had more than one prowler on their hands."

"What about George Pierson?" I asked. "Shouldn't the landlord get more scrutiny as well as the tenants and owners?"

"Yes. I'll check him out, although it wouldn't surprise me if someone at the Sheriff's Department has already done that, too. How much do you know about him, Marty?"

"Not much more than I already shared with you. He's never done anything that I regarded as suspicious, but to be sure that he's on the up and up, why not check him out? Maybe Scheherazade dislikes him for a reason."

"If he's mixed up in whatever's going on in the Shakespeare Cottage that would explain why he hasn't already installed a surveillance camera—on the porch and patio if not inside the house. He also seemed to dismiss Robyn's concerns quickly." I ate a bite of the luscious strawberry cake that always makes me feel like it's spring, no matter what time of the year it is. The breezy feeling it gave me carried a new question with it. "Robyn's not the first tenant in the cottage; is she the first one to complain about Shakespeare's ghost barging in on her?"

"I don't recall everyone who rented that cottage before Robyn. Dottie Harris was a tenant for a while before she bought the O'Connor Cottage next door to you, wasn't she, Charly?"

"That's entirely possible. It's been several years since she moved in next door. I never asked her which cottage she rented, and she never said a word to me about anything odd going on while she was a tenant. Dottie did appear concerned when I spoke to her today, though. Why not? The police lights woke her in the middle of the night, and I told her we'd had a prowler on the loose in the neighborhood. I didn't say that it had anything to do with the Shakespeare Cottage."

"Ask her about it. If she did rent the cottage, maybe she saw Shakespeare's ghost." Marty leaned over and set her plate on the edge of the coffee table. Out of the corner of my eye, I saw Scheherazade running with her belly low to the ground. I lost track of her until I felt her soft fur brush against my leg as she dashed under the coffee table.

"That's exactly what I'll do. I'm going to stop by and see how she's doing when I get home. I'll take her a piece of this amazing cake, which will put her in a talkative mood. I'm sure I'll crash when the sugar rush drops me, but right now, I'm not the least bit sleepy. Even if Dottie didn't have any encounters with intruders, she might know who rented the cottage before or after she did, and we can get the name of another former tenant," Charly said.

A big white paw reached up from under the coffee table. The first time Scheherazade whacked the table with it, she missed Marty's plate. Before I could get the words out of my mouth, the furry princess struck again. This time Marty's dessert plate and fork flipped onto the floor. We all startled. Not just at the clanging of items hitting the tile floor, but the doorbell rang, too.

7

Who's There?

"Knock, knock, knock! Who's there?"
—Macbeth

∞

"WHO'S THERE?" I hollered as if I were at home in my Hemingway Cottage. My heart was pounding wildly. I'd jumped to my feet as Marty dove for the floor to start cleaning gooey pink crumbs from the fluffy white rug. Scheherazade licked her paw and hissed before flouncing away again.

"Princess doesn't approve," I observed as I picked up my plate and headed for the door.

"Either she's not a fan of strawberries or she doesn't approve of the fact that I wouldn't share," Marty said.

"I'll get the door." I set my plate on the gleaming stone counter in Marty's kitchen on my way. Still wary after our conversation about prowlers and ghosts and smugglers, I peeked through the peephole. I removed the chain from the door and yelled so the others could hear me. "It's Robyn!"

"Hello, Miriam. I know I missed dinner. Am I too late

for dessert? Do you have enough for Detective Miller who was kind enough to escort me here?" I opened the door wide and tried not to say or do anything stupid as I invited them in. Hank's car was parked at the curb; his eyes were parked on me.

"There's plenty of cake. We can fix you both a plate, too, if you're hungry. We needed comfort food, so it's old-fashioned baked macaroni and cheese. You can have that, or the wonderful salad Marty prepared, or both like the rest of us did." I shut the door behind them as Scheherazade came running down the hall ahead of Marty. She ignored Robyn and went straight for Hank. She was still checking him out when he reached down and swept her up.

"Wow! What a beauty you are," he said holding her in both hands to examine her. I held my breath waiting for her to hiss or swat at him, but she went dishrag limp when he spoke those words. He tucked her into his arms the way you might do with a baby. I could hear her purring from where I stood a foot or so away. "What's her name?"

"Scheherazade—Princess Scheherazade of Chat du Marrakesh, but I just call her Scheherazade or Princess. I also have a few other names for her when she's naughty like she was a few minutes ago."

"Naughty? How could a beautiful princess like this ever be naughty?" The cat blinked her big gold eyes at Hank and snuggled closer.

"She sure likes you," Neely commented as she joined us. "How are you doing, Robyn?"

"Tired, but most of the cleanup is done."

"The locksmith installed new locks, too, and the alarm's been reset," Hank added as he set the cat on the floor. She swished around his legs before trotting over to Marty.

"Someone will come by tomorrow to patch and paint gouges and scrapes on the door, and in the foyer, hallway, and pantry," Robyn said wearily. "My watercolor needs to be reframed, and I've got to restock the pantry, but that can wait a few more days. By the way, Joe called me to tell me to get over here and try the cake. He also said he wants to install cameras, so I already gave out the brand new alarm code. Hank said it was okay."

I glanced at the detective who was eying me again. Maybe he was evaluating the changes in my appearance. I'd splurged on a visit to the salon once we'd received the amazing news that Edgar had sent a check to the HOA and paid our special assessment fees. I'd had it cut, and the gray hair was gone now that I no longer felt I had to hide my age.

Something in his gaze reminded me of the way he'd looked at that cat—appreciative, I suppose. I tried not to go all limp like Scheherazade had done, but I couldn't resist smiling. The blue in his eyes deepened as he returned my smile. Then he addressed Joe's idea of installing cameras.

"It can't hurt to have cameras set up, although I'm not sure what they'll catch on video if you're still convinced your visitor is a ghost." Scheherazade meowed and looked over her shoulder before walking slowly down the hall with her tail held high. We all followed her.

"Sometimes cameras capture images of ghosts if they're

in a fully materialized state," Robyn asserted and then shrugged when he didn't appear to be convinced. "The detective came by to give me updates about what the crime lab has found so far. I thought you'd want to hear it, too. Macaroni, salad, and cake sure sound good to me. All I've had since breakfast was a granola bar."

"It sounds great to me, too. If you don't mind feeding me, I'll share a couple of things we've discovered about what went on in Robyn's cottage. It won't take long since they haven't gone through all the evidence collected overnight." I fought off the impulse purr, but I did feel a little weak in the knees as Hank put his hand on my elbow and walked alongside me.

"Miriam doesn't mind feeding you. You've got to try the dreamy strawberry cake she brought us. It was one of her husband's favorites before he died." I stopped abruptly, feeling as if the wind had been sucked out of me.

"If Peter Webster enjoyed it that much, I'm sure I will too. He seems to have been a man with excellent taste. I'm sorry for your loss, Miriam. A year's not a lot of time to deal with the sudden death of a man to whom you were married for more than a quarter century." My mouth popped open.

"Did you run a background check on me?"

"Of course we did. How else would we have ruled you out as a suspect in Diana Durand's murder so quickly? The rest of these folks have been in the area for years; then you show up, and a few months later, there's a murder, and you find the body. It's always better to be safe than sorry." He tugged at my arm, urging me on toward the kitchen.

In the kitchen, we fixed plates for Hank and Robyn and then all settled in to hear what Hank had to say. It was a tight squeeze at a table that normally seats six, but we made do by dragging an extra chair to the table. When I'd brought a pot of tea to the table and poured cups for us, I noticed that the chair left empty for me was next to Hank. What choice did I have but to sit down—short of creating a scene?

"So, I heard what you and Robyn had to say about putting the cottage back together; what other news did you bring us, Hank?" Charly asked. I was grateful that she'd gotten the ball rolling. Crammed in as we were, Hank and I kept bumping into each other if either of us moved. It was distracting, to say the least.

"The crime lab guys have found odd streaks of a white substance in the pantry. They're still analyzing what it is, but I've already told Robyn that it must have been left by the ghost."

"Ghost dust," Robyn muttered as she swallowed and then went back to eating.

"Does it glow in the dark?" Neely asked. That stopped Hank in his tracks for a moment. Then Neely reminded him about what Charly, and I had seen and filled him in on what she'd already told us about glow paint.

"I'll find out if they found traces of anything like that," he said.

"I've seen it before after Shakespeare visited. It's ghost dust, I tell you."

"We're not disagreeing with you, Robyn, except to say that the ghost is a fake. He's obviously on the hunt for something and wearing the disguise to send you running so he can have his way with your belongings."

"Then how do you explain how he gets into the cottage without setting off alarms or breaking the locks on the doors?" she asked. "You saw him vanish, too, didn't you?" Neely explained how we thought he might have been able to pull that off with the 'cloak of invisibility.' Robyn liked that part.

"I know you've told us no one else was around when Shakespeare paid you a visit but was anyone else ever nearby right before or after The Bard appeared?" I asked.

"Security came by once or twice before they blew me off. And the police. George showed up a couple of times not long after I called him demanding that he rekey the locks," she replied.

"How long did it take him to get there after you called him?" Marty asked.

"Ten or fifteen minutes, maybe. Not three minutes like security, but I was satisfied with his response time. Of course, I quit calling him when the third or fourth time I called he chewed me out about it. I suppose he was ticked off because changing the locks won't keep a ghost out, will it?"

"What is it, Marty?" I asked given the frown that had overcome her.

"George lives just outside of Duneville Downs. I drove back and forth to his house numerous times when we were seeing each other. It never took us less than twenty-five or thirty minutes. Usually, well over thirty minutes, especially during rush hour."

"Does he have other properties he manages in the community or nearby?" Hank asked.

"Maybe. Sure, that must be it. He could have driven to Shakespeare Cottage quickly if he was nearby dealing with another tenant when Robyn called him."

"At ten or eleven at night?" Robyn asked. "Shakespeare's a night owl." It was Hank's turn to wear a big frown.

"Spill it, Hank," Charly demanded. "Please?"

"On the face of it, he comes up clean. Before he retired, George Pierson worked for several different companies that do mining and offshore drilling, starting as a college intern when he was eighteen."

"Marty already gave us the basics about his career as a mining engineer before he retired and became a property manager, so what?"

"His pension is from twenty-five years of service with a large, well-known oil company that was gobbled up by a larger well-known company. When that happened, he took early retirement. That wasn't his last job, though. The last place he worked went belly up under a cloud of suspicion about overselling shares in a speculative mining and oil exploration venture. George Pierson wasn't charged with anything. He was on the technology and natural resource side of the exploration, not in sales, so I didn't make anything of it."

"I still don't see how you can," Charly responded. "You're not trying to say that he's the guy in the ghost getup just because he arrived so soon after Shakespeare left?"

"No, but according to Robyn, he was also the first person to suggest whatever was going on had something to do with a ghost. I'm not sure he told you it was Shakespeare, did he?"

"No. At first, I didn't actually see Shakespeare's ghost. It started with a mist in the hallway. I'm sure that's because Shakespeare was still working on developing his ability to establish his corporeal presence. I've said that already, haven't I?" She paused to switch her empty dinner plate for the smaller dessert plate. "In fact, I asked George if it was possible that Shakespeare was the one roaming around in the cottage since the place is named for him, so that part wasn't his idea."

"Robyn, did the owners leave anything in your cottage?" I asked.

"Besides their furniture and books and paintings, you mean?"

"Are you saying all the furniture and décor belongs to the owners?" Midge asked.

"Not all of it, but the cottage was rented to me 'furnished.' I asked George to put some things into storage so I could bring my favorite chair and a few other items. I liked the idea that it was furnished because I didn't want to move all my furniture out of the condo until I was sure I was serious about becoming a Seaview Cottages resident. My realtor in Fresno tells me I'm more likely to get a buyer with my furniture in place. Once I sell my condo, I'll have to pay for a storage unit here or in Fresno until I can buy a cottage and move in my stuff. So, a furnished cottage is still a good idea."

"That is interesting, isn't it?" I murmured.

"What's interesting?" Marty asked. "That Robyn's renting a furnished place or that I may have been dating a crook? Although I don't get what his past involvement in a phony mining scheme has to do with what's going on in the Shakespeare Cottage."

"My point is that whoever has been snooping around has been pawing through the owners' belongings. That's even more reason to believe this has little to do with you, Robyn, other than the fact that you haven't left despite the attempts to scare you out of your wits."

"Shakespeare has sure taken his good, sweet time searching the place," Midge observed. "Did the lab come up with anything that might shed some light on the culprit's identity or what the heck he's trying to find?"

"George Pierson claims that when Robyn raised her initial concerns that someone had been in the cottage, he went to Ted and Bernadette De Voss and asked them if they'd been in there. They said no. They also told him no when he asked if they wanted to make sure nothing of value had been taken. George says they assured him they took their valuables with them before deciding to rent the cottage. Bernadette De Voss also told him nothing was ever missing even though she'd thought stuff had been moved around while she still lived there."

"By the ghost," Robyn added. Hank nodded.

"Something like that," he said.

"It sounds like George didn't lie to me about the fact that the ghost story originally came from the owner's wife." There was relief in her voice as she made that remark.

"When we saw the items on the floor in the pantry, we talked about the possibility that the burglars were looking for money or jewelry hidden in a box of cereal or a can of baking soda. Here's a new twist based on what was collected at the crime scene and recorded in the investigators' evidence log. Robyn had a shelf full of cookbooks in the kitchen and someone rifled through them. They didn't just shove them out of the way and onto the floor because handwritten notes and recipe cards were strewn all over, too."

"As if someone shook each book before tossing it onto the floor, right?"

"Exactly, Hemingway!" Hank exclaimed. When he looked at me, our eyes met. I felt giddy for a moment as if I might tumble into the cool blue of his eyes in pursuit of the beguiling twinkle in them. When he turned away, I felt as if I'd lost something, but forced myself to pay attention as Charly spoke.

"What that means is the object of their search could be a sheet of paper—a letter, a photo, an invoice or a canceled check—anything that could be slipped in between the pages of a book in addition to being hidden in an ordinary item on a pantry shelf."

"Or in a picture frame behind a painting of sunflowers," Midge added.

"That all makes sense to me. When I first noticed that things had been moved, it was because a picture was crooked on the wall or books on the shelf were rearranged. Drawers that someone had opened weren't completely shut. Little changes like that."

"Some of the vent covers weren't attached properly," Hank added. "George Pierson checked those today when he stopped by, and he says they weren't like that the last time he inspected the property."

"Unless he's come into the cottage unannounced, the

last time he did that was when my lease was up for renewal. That was months ago, so if someone removed and then replaced the vent covers that could have happened long before last night." Robyn paused and then added another comment. "George wasn't in his usual neighborly landlord mood last night. Even when I've annoyed him, he's always been congenial. Maybe, it's something about you, Detective, or he doesn't feel as neighborly toward the police, but he was almost rude at times."

"I don't take it personally," Hank said in a reassuring way. "It's okay to be suspicious about everyone who has anything to do with the cottage. That goes for all of you. I'm urging that you be cautious since I'm not going to dissuade you from sleuthing."

He had that last part right. No one said anything one way or the other, but the resolve was apparent to me in their poker faces and impassive body language. I did share Hank's concern about the need to take precautions.

"It's the trouble last night that makes me the most uncomfortable. It's your stuff someone went through, Robyn, and while this may not have started out being about you, you're in the thick of it now."

"I agree with Miriam," Charly said. "For the next few days, it's better if you don't go near the cottage alone—day or night. Neely's already invited you to stay with her. Please take her up on her offer."

"I couldn't have said it better," Hank added.

"Okay," Robyn agreed.

"Did you ask George Pierson where he was last night?" Neely asked.

"I did," Robyn replied. "I tried to call him, and he didn't pick up the call until this morning. He said he was at the Blue Haven Resort with a friend and had turned off his phone."

"If he's a regular at the resort that could explain how he got to you so quickly when you called him at ten o'clock at night. It's more like ten minutes away—much closer than his place in Duneville Downs." Marty didn't appear to be happy. "Maybe you should haul him in and give him the third degree, Detective. Ask him to tell you who can give him an alibi. I doubt he was there alone."

"That won't be necessary," Hank replied. "I know exactly where he was last night." We waited for Hank to explain, but he abruptly changed the subject. "More cake, please?"

What is going on? I wondered as I got up to cut another piece of cake for him. Were Hank and Darnell at the resort when they responded so quickly to the call past midnight about a prowler at Seaview Cottages? Was Hank tracking George Pierson's whereabouts in connection to the smuggling case he was working on? Did that have anything to do with what was going on in the Shakespeare Cottage?

8

Tomorrow, and Tomorrow, and Tomorrow

"To-morrow, and to-morrow, and to-morrow,
creeps in this petty pace from day to day."
—Macbeth

∞

I WANTED TO ask my questions, although I didn't believe Hank would respond to questions about an ongoing investigation. I didn't want to get Charly into any trouble since I don't believe we were even supposed to know there was a smuggling investigation underway. Charly interceded before I could stew about it anymore.

"I hate to break this up, folks, but I need to call it a night. We all have plenty to do tomorrow, and I need to go check on my neighbor. Emily still needs to go for a walk. I'll bet Domino does, too, doesn't she?"

"Yes, she does." I handed Hank another piece of cake which he dug into immediately.

"You need to take some of the cake to Dottie. Let me get a little container to put it in." Marty pulled several containers out of the cupboard. "I'm sure the detective would take some home with him for tomorrow if you insist, Miriam."

"No insistence required. I could eat this cake tomorrow, and tomorrow, and tomorrow."

"Aha! Another Shakespeare fan has revealed himself in the kitchen of your Fitzgerald Cottage," Midge said.

"I can't say that's always been true, but when I went to the Bay Area about another case I'm working on, a colleague insisted I go to a new outdoor theater in wine country. The Calla Lily Vineyard Players performed Macbeth using some interesting sets and visual effects."

"Nothing too exotic or avant-garde, I hope," Midge asserted. "I'm not a purist, but Shakespeare is plenty over-the-top without having to add eerie music or too much fire and brimstone."

"No, but now I wish I'd asked questions about how they pulled off some very convincing ghostly effects," Hank said.

"It's not all that mysterious on a set with smoke and mirrors," Neely said, yawning as she stood up to leave. "We all need to catch up on our sleep. It was past two in the morning when Robyn and I got home. Today's been rough even on a devout night owl like me."

"You know from what Neely's already told us, it wouldn't be too surprising if your crime scene investigators turned up a few smears of glow in the dark greasepaint. Especially if the quarreling Robyn heard got physical, and the guy in the windbreaker shoved Shakespeare into a wall or a doorway," I suggested. Neely nodded.

"If Shakespeare and his arch enemy took their brawl into the pantry, bravo to the crime lab if they can find anything by going through that mess." Marty was bustling around and, with Midge's help, rapidly returning her kitchen to the pristine condition it had been in when we arrived for dinner.

"They can sometimes work a bit of magic," Hank responded. "We have a few fresh prints to run, in addition to the handprint left at the front door. Maybe we'll get lucky, and the prints will turn up in the database, and when we go to question the person they belong too, he'll be wearing a windbreaker and sporting a broken nose."

"At least we know how that intruder got out of the house. Did you have any luck figuring out Shakespeare's escape route?" I asked.

"The sliders and the door leading from the kitchen to the garage were locked. The garage door can be locked from the outside, so someone with a key could have left that way," Hank replied.

"That's true. The key Robyn gave us not only unlocks the door leading from the kitchen to the garage but the one from the garage to the back yard. I couldn't get over the six-foot fence, but maybe the cluck in a Shakespeare suit could," Neely suggested.

"Once you'd bashed that guy in the head and wandered off in a daze, the front door was still open. The easiest way to escape would have been for Shakespeare to exit that way, too," Charly said.

"If there are keys floating around that have fallen into the wrong hands, they're useless now that all the locks have been changed. I can't think of another way to get into the house unless Robyn's right and Shakespeare can pass through walls."

"If that happens, maybe we'll catch him in the act on video. I'm going to have a chat with my old dirt-loving boyfriend who ought to know the ins and outs of the cottage better than anyone does. He'd better not turn up on that video footage if he knows what's good for him." As Marty said that, I handed Hank the cake I'd boxed for him.

"Thanks, Hemingway," Hank said. "You still owe me cookies, I believe." I nodded.

"I know. It's on my to-do list." I'd felt awkward about seeing him again since I wasn't sure how to set the record straight after misleading him about my marital status. Now that I knew he'd run that background check on me, I had no excuse.

"I'm sure if anything turns up on the video once Joe gets it set up, you'll call me. That's especially true if it turns out to be George Pierson, okay?"

"With pleasure," Marty said. "That rat's going down if he's behind any of this."

Two minutes later, I left Marty's house. As exhausted as I was, I'd had trouble falling asleep. I was wired after the stress of wrestling with Robyn's problems at the cottage. My interactions with Hank Miller were also stressful. When I awoke, my mind was still awash in conflicted feelings about the man. Despite my curiosity about him and the attraction I felt, I couldn't decide if I wanted to get to know him better.

"Maybe I'm still angry with Pete about dropping dead," I muttered as I climbed out of bed. Domino made the funny sound she sometimes makes that's a cross between a yawn and a whine. "I know that wasn't his fault, but he kept so much from us. I'm not sure I'm ready to trust another man—even one sworn to uphold the law."

After a year on my own, there were aspects of my new life that I'd come to appreciate. It was a relief not to have to accommodate Pete's wishes all the time or worry about being home, on the dot, to fix dinner. Or feel guilty because I didn't get everything done on my to-do list, like baking those cookies for the detective.

"Mama's grumpy this morning, Domino. How about I accommodate your wish for a morning walk?" She woofed, jumped up onto the bed, roughed up the sheets a little, and then ran to get her leash. "Heck, what's so bad about making wishes come true for your fellow creatures?"

Not only did the walk make Domino happy, it also cleared my head. When we returned, I stood on the porch savoring the fresh morning breeze. From the porch, I gazed at the lazy waves rolling onto shore. The sunlight glittered with promise, but the vastness of the horizon made me feel small and insignificant. It might be nice to have someone in my life who regarded me as special. Perhaps sensing my mood, Domino nuzzled my hand that still held onto her leash.

"You think I'm special, don't you? Let's go find food!"

I'd just finished breakfast when my phone rang. I recognized Marty's number, and a wave of apprehension swept over me at the thought of talking to George Pierson. I couldn't shake the feeling that he was involved in something underhanded and the police had him under scrutiny for a good reason. Marty was determined to speak with George and had called him as soon as we'd gone home.

"He seemed glad to hear from me, amiable and polite. Thanks to Hank, now that I know more about George, he came across as a little too amiable. There was something insincere in his tone. When I asked him to have lunch with us to give us more background about the Shakespeare Cottage, he said he'd love to. Then he started making excuses about why he couldn't do it."

"Like what?" I asked as I refilled my coffee cup.

"He'd have to check his other appointments, and he wasn't sure he could get away while the repair people were supposed to be there all day. Please! If he couldn't get away because workers were going to be there all day, what difference did it make if he had other appointments?"

"Robyn and Neely will be there, won't they?" I asked.

"Yes."

"Robyn isn't supposed to be there alone, but I don't see why they can't hold down the fort long enough for him to join us for lunch here."

"I don't get it either except that he's being evasive. Now I wonder how often he did that—appeared to be agreeable and then wiggled out of things. Maybe that's the reason our relationship didn't go anywhere, and it wasn't about dirt at all."

"So, what's the plan?"

"I suggested we bring lunch to him and dine al fresco on Robyn's patio. By then, I was wise to him and headed him off at the pass before he raised objections about sitting down to chat over lunch with paint fumes and hammering going on around us. He hemmed and hawed before agreeing to do it. I can make potato salad if you can bring sandwiches."

"How about chicken, with bow-tie pasta, a pasta casserole, or sesame noodles? Deviled eggs would be good,
too. He's not a vegetarian or lactose intolerant or anything
like that, is he?"

"The old carnivore eats like a horse. As far as I can
recall, that includes anything you put in front of him. In
fact, what finally won him over was my argument that he
had to eat. If he couldn't go out for lunch, why not let us
bring lunch to him? He's a sucker for potato salad, and
I'm not ashamed to say I offered it as a covert attempt at
bribery. All your suggestions are wonderful. I'll also pack
plates and eating utensils, a table cloth for outdoors—all
the things we'll need like that, including a bottle of
George's favorite white wine."

"We should bring enough to feed Robyn and Neely,
too."

"That's fine, although I'd rather interrogate George
without Robyn sitting there. I don't want him worrying
that what he tells us will contradict what he's already told
Robyn. Not that I believe he's regarded her of much
consequence until this latest incident. If it isn't too stinky
or noisy, we can set up lunch for them in the study. Neely
might prefer that if she's hard at work on her laptop
digging into the history of the old house and the De Voss
family. We'll make it work."

"Did you agree on a time?"

"Two, which is later than I normally eat lunch, but I
would have said yes to any time he suggested. I'm determined to corner this guy and ask him a few pointed
questions about the cottage. He knows more about what's

going on there than he's willing to say. It wouldn't surprise me, in fact, if he's up to no good."

"Up to no good, how?" I asked even though I'd had almost the same thoughts about him.

"Hank's no dummy, but neither am I. You don't have to read through the lines too deeply to see that the police are more than a little interested in George Pierson. What if the dirt snoop in George has discovered the area around the cottage or under it is loaded with a rare mineral? Or more likely, what if all the coming and going in the Shakespeare Cottage is related to the smuggling and George is covering for it?"

"I don't want to jump to conclusions about a man I've never met, but my mind wandered down the same path last night when I should have been sleeping."

"Jump all you want. I can't believe I didn't catch on to what an unsavory character he is even after Princess tried to warn me. I'll never doubt her again."

"They would have made lots more noise than they already have if they were storing smuggled goods in Robyn's garage or attic crawl space, and then sending someone to haul them away later."

"I hear you, Miriam. If they were using her garage to hide smuggled loot, why would Shakespeare's ghost, or anyone else, bother to go into the house at all? You have access to the attic from out there, too. Besides, you're right, she's never said a word about hearing footsteps overhead."

"If they're passing each other little notes by hiding them in books or behind paintings in the cottage, why go to so much trouble?" I asked. "That can't be it either."

"Good grief, I agree. Stick the note under a potted plant on the porch and ditch the Shakespeare's ghost getup! Or leave the notes in books at the public library."

"Okay, bye for now. I'm going to call Neely to tell her about lunch." As I said that, I was already examining the contents of my pantry to see what I had on hand to fix for an al fresco lunch for five.

"Neely," I said the moment she picked up the phone.

"Miriam? Is everything okay?"

"So far, but it's still early."

"I can tell. I haven't had coffee yet, but I smell it. That must mean Robyn's up already. Despite my misgivings that nothing good happens before ten o'clock, we agreed to get to the cottage by nine to see what's up today." I heard a crash and then a yelp. "Stubbed my toe, dang it. I left my glasses next to my reading chair where I was working on my laptop. That'll teach me not to put them next to the bed. I'm blind as a bat. What's up?"

"Marty and I wanted to talk to you about lunch." I quickly filled her in about the arrangements we'd made with George Pierson and our preference to question him without Robyn being at the table.

"That makes sense. He's not above contradicting himself, that's for sure. If she isn't sitting there to correct him, I doubt he'll worry about it."

"Marty's concerned that he's deceitful—says yes, does no—although she didn't realize that when they were dating."

"Scheherazade didn't miss it, did she? That cat has an attitude, but she might be on to something when it comes to George Pierson." I'd already reconsidered my opinion of the cat after seeing how she'd taken a shine to Hank. I suddenly felt uncomfortable about how much Scheherazade disliked George Pierson.

"I wonder what George did to Scheherazade to make her dislike him so much that she hisses at the mere mention of his name."

"Neely!" I heard a voice say after what sounded like a rap on the door.

"Uh, oh, Robyn's hollering. Hang on."

"I'm up," Neely said as she opened the door to her room. "I've got Miriam on the phone planning what to bring us for lunch at your cottage if we're still there at two."

"Please tell Miriam thanks. I hope we'll be out of there by then, but you never can tell. Breakfast will be ready in two minutes—eggs and toast, but no grits. Those were dumped on the floor in my pantry and I don't see any in yours." I made a mental note to take deviled eggs off the list of my lunch options.

"Mm, I smell bacon, too. I'll be right there." The door clicked shut.

"It's not always bad to share your digs with someone else, is it? If you all keep feeding me, though, I'm going to lose my girlish figure." Neely cackled at her joke. I was about to say goodbye when I wondered about what she'd said earlier.

"What did George say to contradict himself?" I asked.

"Several small things. When George was speaking to the painters over the phone, he told them the house was twenty-eight hundred square feet in size. Robyn says she reminded him that the realtor claims it's twenty-one hundred square feet. He'd also used the smaller number before. He was contracting for touch-up work, not a whole house paint job, so it didn't matter. It's a big difference in size, isn't it? Hank told Robyn that George couldn't seem to come up with the same story twice about her reports of incidents at the cottage. When we got home last night, I asked her to sit down and recount as many incidents as she could and attach the dates. That didn't take long. Apparently, Robyn's been keeping a ghost diary."

"She has a log of events?"

"Yep! In her case, Shakespeare should have written something about yesterday, and yesterday, and yesterday, huh?"

"Did she give a copy to Hank?"

"I don't think so, but I can ask her."

"Tell Charly about it and ask her what we should do about it. I wonder if those dates will mean anything to Hank and the other investigators tracking the movement of the smugglers."

"Maybe, they ought to be taking a closer look at the owners of the cottage, too. It wouldn't be the first time a member of the De Voss family was involved in smuggling. In fact, it appears to be an old family tradition, along with the curse and ghost stories."

"What does that mean, Neely?"

9

Eat and Drink as Friends

"And do as adversaries do in law, strive mightily,
but eat and drink as friends."
—Taming of the Shrew

∞

"I FOUND SEVERAL more sources that referred to the De Voss family's involvement in rum-running in the South Bay area during Prohibition. That activity was centered around LA and San Diego even though the family already owned Seaview Bluffs Manor. They paid a price for their misdeeds, although they were notoriously brutal in defense of their dirty work. In the 1920s, during Prohibition, two of Rupert and Hilda's adult sons drowned when their boat, loaded with liquor they were bringing into the country from Mexico, sank."

"Two more gruesome deaths. At least they didn't die at home, but I can understand why there was so much talk about a curse and restless spirits."

"The family's past came back to haunt them years later. When Frederick De Voss ran for mayor of Duneville Down right before the end of World War II, he was skewered in the local press. They claimed the money he was using to bankroll his campaign came from bootlegging and other illicit activities. That put a damper on his political aspirations, but they ended for good when he was killed a few months later in a hail of bullets."

"That's straight out of a gangster movie!" I exclaimed.

"It sure was. Freddie De Voss was gunned down as he climbed into his limo parked in front of his house. That wasn't more than a few days after he'd hosted a wild party that included Hollywood celebrities, writers, artists, a few bankers, and, supposedly, a couple of bigwigs tied to organized crime."

"Cavorting with members of the mob must have added fuel to the fire for anyone claiming the De Voss family's wealth came from illegal activities."

"You can say that again, Miriam. The scuttlebutt was that Freddie paid for an old score he'd attempted to settle by wining and dining mob members. His murder also set off a round of gossip about the return of the Hempstead Towers curse. It wasn't the deceased Hempsteads, but poor Freddie's ghost locals reported wandering on the bluff or down below on the beach."

"Robyn doesn't know about any of this, does she?" As if on cue, I heard Robyn calling Neely's name again.

"I'm on my way, Robyn!" Neely shouted before answering my question.

"No, she doesn't, and I intend to keep it that way for now. She's jumpy enough already. Last night before she went to bed, she shut all the blinds, checked all the locks on the doors, and asked me two or three times if I'd set the alarm. I'm not sure what scares her most now, ghosts or real people."

"If George Pierson or someone else had done something six months ago, she might be in better shape. She's never going back to that cottage unless we solve this mystery. I'll help her break the lease if it comes to that. In another week or so, I'll also take her to look at the cottages that are for sale."

"That should get her refocused. She needs to be thinking more about tomorrow, and tomorrow, and tomorrow. Someone's going to snap up her condo in Fresno any minute now and she ought to have a plan in place."

"It occurred to me last night that she might be able to work out a rent-to-own deal with someone eager to sell. All the money she pays for rent could go toward the purchase of her home."

"Wouldn't that be great not to put more money into a place that's not hers?"

"And that she has to share with Shakespeare and who knows who else? Let's see what Midge has to say about the realtor who's taken Greta Bishop's place."

"Okay, see you at two—where we'll 'strive mightily, but eat and drink as friends.' Shakespeare was full of great ideas, wasn't he?"

"It sounds good. Let's see how well it works."

The morning flew by as I did my usual chores, made a cheesy, ziti pasta casserole for lunch, and baked cookies. I planned to make good on that promise to Hank. If potato salad worked as a covert bribe with George Pierson, why not cookies, too?

While the cookies baked, I engaged in a little armchair snooping. I pored over every bit of information I could find about the Shakespeare Cottage. I wanted to arm myself with as much background as I could uncover before facing the man who markets and manages the place on behalf of the current owners.

The parcel of land and the cottage on it, were exempt from any and all assessments levied on Seaview Bluff Manor and any subsequent property built in its place. The developers of the Seaview Cottages Active Adult Community had also agreed to pay the property taxes from the point at which the family sold the property until it was fully developed and completely sold out.

As far as I could tell, that meant the De Voss family got a free ride on taxes for three decades and were still saving thousands each year on assessments. Exactly how much they were saving wasn't clear. Assessments are based, in part, on the square footage of the homes built in our community. I'll be darned if I could get an exact figure for how large Shakespeare Cottage is. The disagreement about it was much like the figures being disputed by Robyn and her landlord—ranging from just under three thousand square feet to less than two thousand.

I found old floor plans for the cottages the developers built, and none of them came close to the three thousand square foot mark. Homes that big are commonplace now, but in the sixties and seventies, houses half that size were considered roomy. When I tried to find information on the county tax assessor website using the owners' names, parcel number, and the street address, I had no luck.

I'd worked my way through all the online archived material first and then switched to a box of file folders and odd-sized manila envelopes. I'd brought these materials home a week or so ago when I'd received the news that the Executive Committee had officially passed the eighty/twenty rule that made me a legal resident of the community at age fifty. I was so relieved that I probably would have agreed to scrub all the toilets in the clubhouse for the next year if they'd asked me to do it.

Instead, I'd agreed to sort and catalog this stuff—there was more, too, but I'd decided to start with the oldest documents first. Stopping every few minutes to take cookies out of the oven and put more in, I plowed through stacks of paper including old handbills for community events, faded polaroid photos, menus for holiday celebrations, newspaper clippings, awards that had been given out or received that were probably meant to be on display somewhere, and an opening day announcement.

The items seemed to be organized by year. When I got to 1971, I sucked in my breath when I read the headline on the front page of the Duneville Downs Daily: "**A new Tragedy for one of our oldest families.**" The article was short. Daniel De Voss, young, hip, good-looking in a seventies sort of way, had died of a drug overdose. Suicide had not been ruled out. In his twenties, the young man was reportedly bereft at the disappearance of his wife, Constance, who friends and family called Cookie.

"What do you think about that, Domino? I haven't heard of anyone called Cookie in years, and in two days, the name pops up twice. Maybe it doesn't count since it's George's dog, and not a family member named Cookie." Domino jumped up and barked sharply as if she didn't quite buy that argument. "Okay, I take it back. Dogs count, too! Cookie De Voss was a looker, don't you agree?" I showed Domino the photo I'd found.

Cookie De Voss looked a lot like Marlo Thomas in *That Girl*, although Cookie's makeup was more dramatic. Domino stepped forward and looked at the photo, gave the newsprint a sniff and then barked loudly. Usually, I have a hunch or can concoct a way to interpret Domino's response to my queries, but this time I was lost. I sniffed the newsprint, and that didn't help. It smelled musty as you might expect for a paper that was half a century old.

Had they ever found Cookie De Voss? If so, where? When? Did she know that her husband had died—maybe at his own hand because she'd gone missing? I was digging through the box of materials hoping I might find answers to my questions. When the timer on the oven pinged, I yelped. Domino yelped in reply. I know when I'm being mocked and laughed at Domino's silliness and mine.

When I pulled the last batch of cookies out of the oven to cool, I had a sudden inspiration. Marty's reference to George as an old carnivore suddenly made me rethink my food as bribery strategy. I double-checked the time.

"It'll be close, but we can do it, Domino." I pulled a lovely beef tenderloin from the fridge that I'd bought for my contribution to one of our upcoming potlucks. "This isn't enough for a main dish for five, but it'll wow him as an appetizer won't it?" I hit the button on my stereo system, and music poured out around me as I picked up the pace. A little over an hour later, I'd loaded a trolley with my goodies and set off on foot for the Shakespeare Cottage. Since we were eating outdoors, I didn't see any reason not to bring along Domino. She was prancing!

When we arrived at the cottage, the place was buzzing

with activity. I'd called Marty who agreed to meet me at the side gate and let me into the back yard. She was bubbling like a socialite at a coming out party. I hoped it was an act, but I wasn't so sure by the way she made a fuss over George Pierson. As Marty introduced me to George, a shy, blond cocker spaniel touched noses with Domino. Cookie stepped back for a second until Domino crouched down and then took off. Cookie followed at a prudent distance but carried a doggie toy with her that she and Domino soon shared.

The yard was enormous and gave me a much better appreciation for the cottage's 'footprint.' The larger estimate of its size had to be the correct one. The view of the golf course and clubhouse made me realize that Shakespeare Cottage, while not on a hilltop was situated on an elevated lot.

"It's nice to meet you," I said trying to sound as though I meant it. George looked nothing like I'd ex-pected. From Marty's description of him as an old carnivore who'd spent years on oil rigs and in rough terrain searching for mining opportunities, I'd figured he'd be a big, burly, muscular man.

Wiry, with a ruddy complexion and sparse reddish hair on top of his head, it was immediately apparent to me that George Pierson wasn't likely to be our Shakespeare impersonator. Not without considerable padding and maybe even lifts in his shoes. Of course, the disguise was intended to deceive, so perhaps it had been made to add weight and height to the person wearing it. Besides, we'd only seen the ghostly mime for a minute or less and at a distance.

"My pleasure, although I'm not sure what I can tell you that can add any clarity to Robyn's puzzling situation."

"Oh, let's not get down to business quite yet. I'm dying to see what Miriam has brought us. She's such a great cook, and I've never met a better baker in my life. Why don't we set out the goodies you brought, and then make sure we take care of Neely and Robyn who are holding down the fort inside. Robyn's there to answer questions while Neely works on a project with a deadline she's trying to meet." As she made that last comment, Marty gave me a little wink.

"Neely always has some new project, doesn't she?" I said in a lighthearted tone.

"Our appetizer," I said as I removed foil from a platter that contained slices of beef tenderloin on a bed of arugula drizzled with an herby red wine sauce. The aroma swirled around us. George Pierson, who'd stood during the introductions, sat back down.

"That does look good. I thought we might be eating nothing but salad since this wasn't a cookout and women seem to survive on weeds and grass." He guffawed.

A man who appreciates his own humor, I thought, making eye contact for a second with Marty. With her back to George, she rolled her eyes. When I placed the baked ziti casserole next to the appetizer, his eyes widened.

"Main course," I said. "And, dessert! I hope you're not one of those people who shies away from sugar."

"Not me. Marty can tell you that I've ordered more than one dessert, on occasion, when I couldn't make up my mind which one sounded best. Is it okay to dig in?"

"Please, go ahead. I'm going to take food to Neely and Robyn, and then I'll join you. Will you pour me a glass of wine, George?"

"Gladly! I've died and gone to heaven lunching with two gorgeous women who eat meat and sugar and drink wine." I smiled as if basking in the compliment as I let myself into the kitchen using the sliding doors. I spotted Neely and Robyn, who were seated at a table in a formal dining room. I caught a whiff of paint, but otherwise, it wasn't bad inside at all. Somewhere toward the front of the house, I heard men talking.

"I've brought food for you." I placed containers of food I'd packed for them on the table in front of them. They looked tiny against the backdrop of the large dining table. "If it's not enough maybe George will share."

"We've already been eating chips and seven-layer dip Marty gave us," Neely said pointing to chips and dip alongside a small bowl of potato salad. When I opened the containers, Neely looked over her shoulder. "We'd better eat before the workmen in the foyer get a look at this or we may be outside begging for leftovers." Robyn nodded.

"I'm taking no chances." She began filling a plate as I turned to leave.

"By the way, I've also been following up on the information you sent to Charly and me. So far, I've only found a little more about the woman you were looking for, and I've found nothing to suggest she ever turned up again." I glanced at Robyn who seemed to be oblivious to what we were talking about. "Charly's following up using her special relationships, so maybe she'll get the scoop." I nodded.

"That would be great," I said.

"Joe and Carl stopped by and told us they didn't find anything on the videos they recorded, but maybe Shakespeare is waiting for things to quiet down a little before he returns." I wasn't quite sure what Robyn meant. Staying away while the place you'd burgled was still crawling with people seemed like a no-brainer. Could she possibly still imagine the place was haunted? Neely and I both appeared to be at a loss for words.

"Don't worry, you two, I'm not still insisting there's a real ghost roaming around. On the other hand, I'm trying to keep an open mind. People are tricky, but ghosts are trickier." She shrugged. "Thanks for bringing us food. I fixed us a big breakfast in case we got stranded here all day, so a late lunch is perfect."

"Enjoy!" I said as I left. When I returned to the back yard, I seated myself across from the man who was refilling his empty plate. Marty was doing the same with his wine glass. The eating and drinking were well underway. To borrow a phrase that was around long before Shakespeare, would our 'friend' give up the ghost if he'd been holding out on us?"

10

Doth Protest Too Much

"The lady doth protest too much, methinks."
—Hamlet

∞

"YOU'D BETTER HURRY up and help yourself to lunch before I make my way back to the appetizer. Marty did not exaggerate when she praised your cooking."

"Thank you," I replied as I put food on a plate. "I'm glad the trouble here hasn't spoiled your appetite. It must be more than an inconvenience for a man as busy as you are. Marty says you manage rental properties all over the area—including properties at the Blue Haven Resort."

Marty glanced at me sideways since she hadn't said anything about him managing resort properties. I was fishing for any connection he might have to the nearby resort, and it worked. I paid careful attention to every word he said as I ate heartily.

"Marty thinks I work too hard. She could be right. I'm thinking about scaling back and maybe even taking a little time off to travel. I don't let the job get to me, and I've managed properties where the guests have done lots worse damage than the intruders did here. The Blue Haven realty folks know better than to blame me for it, although they do expect a quick turnaround to get the property back into rentable condition. I have almost zero contact with the homeowners there since most of the properties are timeshares rather than private residences like this one."

"George is being polite, Miriam. The members of the De Voss family aren't always the easiest people to work for. They want the work done fast, just like at the resort, but they call the shots about who can do the repair work."

"Hey, no sweat! Why not hire people who are already familiar with the property? Who wants to worry about some lowlife taking unauthorized photos of the interior or selling stories to the tabloids about cleaning up after a ghost? The family has always been high profile. They've learned to take precautions. I do careful screening before accepting someone as a tenant. Why wouldn't they do the same with the maintenance personnel they hire?"

"I can't imagine all the properties you manage have errant ghosts as troublemakers, do they?" I asked. He laughed and swigged down the wine in his glass. The wine was excellent, but I'd almost done a spit take when I saw the label. At sixty dollars a bottle, George Pierson's good taste costs a pretty penny.

"Fortunately, no! One haunted house is more than enough." He said as he filled his glass and then paused to gaze at me. "You're not serious, are you? I'm afraid I set off the ghost thing when Robyn first called me insisting that someone had been in the cottage even though nothing had been taken. She wanted to call the police, but to report what crime? Eventually, she tried, and they scoffed at her."

"When was that?" Marty asked.

"I'm not sure, but it came up before she renewed her lease almost a year ago. Who renews a lease on a house if they seriously believe someone's breaking in and going through their stuff?" He shrugged. That time frame jived with what Robyn had told us. I helped myself to a cookie and shoved the plate closer to him as I spoke.

"Have previous tenants complained about ghosts? I'm doing a little scrapbooking for the HOA, and I've come across a few things about the property that suggests the ghost stories aren't new."

"That's true. The family has been haunted by them— the stories, I mean, not the ghosts. That's not too funny, is it?" Marty skillfully changed the subject as George inhaled a cookie and then reached for another one.

"I remember you told me that one reason the owners don't live here is that the wife's uncomfortable about the ghost stories. I suppose if you're in this big house and you've heard all the stories, that it's easy to start imagining things. Shame on you for putting such an idea into Robyn's head."

"I regret it now." He picked up another cookie and waved it at us for emphasis. "No one needs to put anything into a De Voss family member's head. They've lived through the incidents that created the stories. So, if Bernadette De Voss doesn't want to live here, who could blame her?" For a minute, George stopped eating and talking and grew pensive. "Guilt does wicked things to the imagination," he muttered almost to himself.

Whose guilt? I wondered. Marty had a puzzled expression on her face and shrugged ever so slightly when we made eye contact.

"To answer your earlier question, yes, other tenants have raised concerns about items being moved around. Like Robyn's situation, nothing ever went missing which made it hard to get worked up about their concerns. The house is big. Both the heat and AC are powerful, so I figured that accounted for some of the stuff people found on the floor." Then he smiled at Marty. "If they had that big, spoiled cat of yours around they'd know who was responsible, wouldn't they?"

"How big is the house, by the way? I'm just curious because the numbers in the HOA materials bounce around so much."

"I've seen the blueprints, and the cottage is almost three thousand square feet. Nothing close to the estate home that was torn down which was huge. Eight bedrooms rather than four like this one. Most of them had their own bathrooms which was unusual when the house was built at the turn of the century. Indoor plumbing, electricity, and a thermal ventilation system using cellars or a crawl space under the house. The place ought to have been preserved rather than demolished."

"How did Shakespeare get mixed up in this?" I wondered aloud.

"That's new, as far as I can tell. Maybe that's my fault, too—the power of suggestion to a susceptible tenant renting a cottage bearing his name. Being in the Shakespeare Cottage meant a lot to her."

"It's more than the power of suggestion now, isn't it?"

I asked. "Robyn's not the only one who's seen a ghostly white figure that bears a striking resemblance to the cottage's namesake."

"He glows in the dark, too," Marty added explaining what Charly and I had seen on our way to Robyn's cottage when she'd called us for help. "According to Robyn, he brought along a sparring partner on his last visit."

"So I've heard," George said.

"What do you make of the break-in. How did the intruders get in?"

"The police detective asked me the same thing, and I'll tell you what I told him—I don't know. If I had to guess, I'd say Robyn is so stressed out that she doesn't know if she's coming or going. Maybe she thought she set the alarm but forgot. Or put in the wrong code and didn't notice. The system gives you an error message, but it doesn't bleep at you like your car does if you leave the keys in the ignition."

"Did she leave the front door unlocked, too?" I asked.

"It's possible, but it's more likely someone got a copy of the key. Before you get upset because you think I'm blaming your friend, it could have been my key. We've had a few trusted repair people in since we last rekeyed the place, so it's possible one of them wasn't as trustworthy as we thought and made a copy." I nodded, letting go of some of the animosity that had welled up in me toward him.

"That's always a problem isn't it?" Marty asked. "You put up gates, bolt the doors, set alarms, but you've still got to let strangers in to do all the maintenance and repair work."

"Tell me about it," George said. "I lose rental pro-
spects sometimes because they don't like the idea that the
golf course and clubhouse are open to the public. I know
the community needs the revenue, but it's another problem
for security here."

"Whoever was in the Shakespeare Cottage left a huge
mess behind, so maybe the police will figure out the
identity of one or both of the burglars," Marty said.

"The detective I spoke to yesterday seemed sharp. He's
motivated to find the culprit since, as he explained it to
me, this wasn't just a burglary, but an assault. Your friend
Neely's a tough cookie. The guy she head-butted got more
than he bargained for, didn't he?" That made me smile.

"That'll teach him to diss his elders," Marty added and
laughed. "Although I guess we don't know how old he
was, do we?" Domino and Cookie stopped playing and
walked over to where we sat on the patio. George's
reference a moment ago to Neely being a tough cookie
already had my mind headed down the track to the death
of Daniel De Voss and the disappearance of Constance De
Voss. The soulful eyes of the cocker spaniel somehow
triggered the image of the beautiful young woman who'd
vanished years ago.

"So, what happened to Cookie De Voss? Did anyone
ever find her?" I asked just as someone opened the sliders
behind me. The dogs ran to greet the visitor as I turned in
my seat to see who it was.

"What business is that of yours?" A woman asked.
"Who are you and what are you doing at my house asking
nosy questions?" I expected George to react in a more
negative way than he did. His employer was obviously

ticked off. I couldn't blame her, but why wasn't he more afraid she was going to fire him right then and there?

"Bernie, this is Marty Monroe, a woman I used to date. The curious one is Miriam Webster—like the dictionary—if that's her real name." Bernie De Voss stepped outside onto the patio, as Domino woofed and then invited her to play.

"Nice to meet you, Ms. De Voss," I said as I stood to greet her. "We're Robyn Chappell's friends and are trying to understand what's going on here before she moves back in. I'm also going through old clippings, trying to organize them so they can be scanned into the community archive as part of our online scrapbooks. I stumbled across the story and wondered what happened to her. I apologize if I triggered unpleasant memories for you, although you can't be old enough to have been around when she went missing in 1971." She might be old enough, but I didn't want to irritate her any further by suggesting she was older than she was, so I quickly calculated that it was better to err by assuming she was younger than she was.

"That's not any of your business, either." She was well-dressed with every hair in place, but she was anxious. Her eyes scanned Marty and me and then darted around the yard.

Why is she so jumpy? I wondered.

"Pull up a chair, and I'll pour you a glass of wine. You should have arrived a few minutes ago before I polished off the last of the beef tenderloin. The casserole is delicious, too. If you've already had lunch, there are cookies..." George stopped speaking. Bernie De Voss's eyes darkened, and she shook her head in exasperation.

"No, no, no! What is your problem? I didn't come here to eat and blab with the neighbors. That's not what you're being paid to do, either!" Then she glared at me before she spoke again.

"I hope the police are more successful in their pursuit of the intruders who ransacked my house than they were when it came to locating Constance De Voss!"

"By intruders do you mean people?" I asked before I could stop myself. "I thought you were a believer in ghosts." She balled up her fists on her hands that were dangling at her sides and stepped closer to me.

"This property is a waste bin of uneasy spirits—most of them are my disturbed husband's disturbed ancestors. You have no idea what's gone on here and why just being here makes my skin crawl!" When she took another step toward me, Domino stepped in between us. Domino didn't growl or bare her teeth, but the jumpy auburn-haired woman shook with rage.

"Get these people out of here before I call Ted and tell him to hire a new property manager!"

"Time to go, ladies," George said as he cleaned up the disposable plates Marty had brought along.

"What about Robyn and Neely?" Marty asked. "Do you want me to get them?"

"I already told them there was no reason to stick around. They left before I realized you two were out here bugging our soon to be ex-property manager." Instead of looking worried, George shook his head and smiled.

"Calm down, Bernie. You know getting this worked up isn't good for your nerves." She stomped around but didn't say anything. In minutes, we'd packed up, and headed out through the gate Domino and I had entered through earlier.

"Well, well, well. Will you look at that! *'The lady doth protest too much, methinks.'*" I glanced back over my shoulder and saw George and Bernie in an embrace.

"How do you like that? What are those two up to?"

"Besides playing her husband for a fool, you mean? That old coot has landed a big fish this time. I'll bet he's about to reel her in, too. No wonder he's thinking about giving up his gig as a property manager to travel!"

"Maybe they're behind all the searching that's going on," I muttered as we walked to the curb where Marty had parked her golf cart. I'd taken her up on her offer to drive us home.

"Then why not just kick out Robyn and go to it? Bernie owns the place. If she doesn't want hubby to know what she's doing, lover boy would search it for her." I nodded agreeing with Marty's point.

"If she and George have plans, they'll have to get past Ted. I can't imagine a De Voss marrying without an airtight prenup, can you? Even if she agrees to the terms of a divorce, Ted may try to fight it. Maybe they're planning to run for it and forget about a divorce."

"In that case, they'd need cash or other things they could turn into cash fast. What if they've been slipping in here to hide money or stock certificates or the family jewels rather than trying to find things?" I shrugged in response to Marty's question.

"I don't know. Let's run this by Charly and see what she has to say. These days, I thought clever thieves just siphoned money into an offshore account. When they had what they thought was enough, they'd hop on a plane or a ship, and head for the Cayman Islands or Thailand." I shrugged again as I issued a command to Domino.

"Get in, Domino! We're going for a ride." I had no problem getting her to agree to that proposition. I doubt her eagerness had anything to do with the anxiety I felt about the need to get away from Bernie De Voss. Marty opened a small storage area on the back and loaded our stuff into it. Then, she folded my cart and wedged it in behind the back seat. As Marty climbed into the driver's seat, I slipped into the passenger's seat. Suddenly, Domino, who was hunkered down on the floor in the seats behind us, stood up and barked, wagging her tail wildly.

"Hello, fellow sleuths. Fancy meeting you here," Carl said as he and Joe pulled up and stopped alongside Marty's cart, facing us driver-to-driver. When Carl used the sleuth word, Marty and I both glanced toward the house. I thought I saw the wood blinds move on the window closest to us.

"Keep it down, will you? We were just leaving," Marty replied. "What's up?"

"We're going to go in and make sure our surveillance cameras are reset and ready to go once this place clears out for the day. I don't see any ladders or trucks. The repair guys must have left."

"You won't go in there until that little roadster is gone if you know what's good for you." Marty nodded her head in the direction of the Porsche sitting at the curb a couple of car lengths behind us. Then she explained what had happened. I had the uncomfortable feeling that we were being watched.

"She may not be done with us yet, if we don't get out of here," I added. "Maybe we should finish catching up when we meet at Midge's house this evening."

"Yeah. You'll have time to come back later to check on the cameras. Just don't break the terms of your deal with Hank." Marty checked the side mirrors and scanned the street, poised to drive off.

"Don't worry; we'll have this golf cart back to the clubhouse before dark. We don't want trouble with the detective. That wouldn't be a very nice thing to do to Miriam now that she's got him hooked on her cookies." Joe burst out laughing, and Carl whooped it up with him.

"Cookies, yeah right!"

"Stop it you guys, or she'll put you under a cookie ban. Then we'll see who's hooked on her cookies, won't we?"

Just then, a car turned onto the street. The driver honked as the car came around the corner. I'm not sure why because even though Joe had parked in an odd way, there was plenty of room to get by. The guy behind the wheel got our attention.

"What's up with that jerk?" Joe asked as the driver drove by slowly and gestured in a most impolite manner. As he did that, the movement of his arm rippled the dark fabric of his windbreaker.

"It must have something to do with the two black eyes and his bandaged nose," Carl replied.

"Okay, so he had a rough night, that's no reason to be a nasty neighbor," Joe added.

"A rough night thanks to Neely Conrad, I bet," I said. "Can you see his license plate number?"

"I sure can," Carl replied. I'd whipped out my phone

and typed in the numbers as he recited them. "I never dreamed I'd have a chance to say it, but follow that car! Don't let him get away."

"Great idea! We promised Hank we wouldn't go out on another ghost patrol or chase the undead. That guy didn't look dead to me." Joe, who was already parked facing the right way to pursue the guy, hit the accelerator pedal.

"Don't worry, we won't pull a Neely on him," Carl added. "We need to see where he's going."

"Yeah, what if the scumbag who attacked Neely is living right under our noses?" Joe called out as he sped off.

"I'm not bailing them out," Marty said. "Not until morning anyway. Spending a night in jail might put a little salt on their tails before they're the ones with the black eyes and broken noses."

"Who should I call first—Hank or Charly?"

"Charly," we said in unison as I hit the quick-dial button for her. When Marty got to the corner, I checked behind us as a car that had been parked across the street slowly pulled away from the curb. Whoever was in that car appeared to be following Joe and Carl.

"Hello."

"Charly, it's Miriam. I think Joe and Carl might be in trouble."

11

Dead as a Doornail

"Yet, come thou and thy five men, and if I do not leave you all as dead as a doornail, I pray God I may never eat grass more."
—Henry VI

∞

"HE'S DEAD! SHAKESPEARE'S ghost is dead!" I hadn't been home long when Robyn called. I'd answered the call, hoping it was Charly with news about Joe and Carl.

"I don't understand. Where are you? Where's Neely?"

"We're back at my cottage. Neely's in the pantry, watching the dead ghost until the police get here. We don't want to lose Shakespeare the way you lost Diana Durand on Fitzgerald's Bluff."

"Okay, so if you've called the police, that's good. What can I do?"

"Come back over here, please. I'm afraid George and that crazy De Voss woman will come back. She's scarier than a ghost or a burglar. When she came in and saw us eating in the dining room, she asked what we were doing.

I told her we were having lunch while the repairmen finished, so I could be sure they did things the way they were supposed to do them. Instead of treating me like I was a responsible tenant, she told me that was her job, not mine. Then she ordered us out. It got a little tense after that."

"I can believe it. Marty and I went through something like that, too."

"Please, come over here, will you? Neely says you ought to have a good look before the police throw us all out. Charly, too!"

"I'm on my way. Domino, leash!" I turned around, and the sweet, clever girl was standing there already carrying her leash. "Well aren't you the savvy pooch?" I grabbed a jacket and took off on foot.

"Charly?" I asked when she answered my call.

"Yes?"

"Here we go again."

"Are you telling me Joe and Carl are in more trouble? I told them to go home. I had to do some fast talking to get Hank to stop the detective who was following them in that car from arresting them."

"No. What did they do?"

"They almost blew a cop's cover who's working on the smuggling investigation."

"Are you saying the guy they were following—the one Neely beat up—is an undercover cop?"

"No, but Eddie Vargas, the driver of the car you saw following them, was trying to hook up with the guy Neely head-butted. The two men were supposed to meet at the clubhouse. Apparently, Carl and Joe spooked him, and he bolted. When the police officer tried to pursue the guy, they got in the way, asking him what his business was in Seaview Cottages. That's when he showed them his badge and called for backup."

"Oh, geez. That's not good." I was starting to huff and puff again. I was hoofing it at top speed, but the increasingly bizarre turn of events didn't help me breathe any easier. Even the undercover meeting seemed odd to me. Why set up a meeting in the vicinity of the Shakespeare Cottage so soon after the incident in which Eddie Vargas' contact came close to being caught as an intruder?

"Even Hank was ready to say, 'off with their heads,' but I reasoned with him that the way those two run their mouths, it would be a bigger risk to put them in jail than to let them go. Anyone within earshot would have quite a story to repeat. I assured Hank that if he told his colleague to release them, I'd keep them from causing another disturbance."

"Uh-oh. That's even more reason to get a move on! Can you grab Emily and come with me to the Shakespeare Cottage?"

"Right now? I was just getting ready to order pizza so we could get to work as soon as you all arrived. What is it?"

"A dead ghost. According to Robyn, Shakespeare's ghost roams no more."

"Good grief. I'll meet you outside in a minute." When she said a minute, she meant it. She and Emily were at the gate by the time Domino and I arrived. During the short walk from the Brontë Cottage to the Shakespeare Cottage, I talked as fast I could. I wanted Charly to know what had gone on today with Bernie De Voss, including the possibility that she was carrying on with George Pierson and the weird interactions several of us had with her.

"It doesn't surprise me that she reacted badly to your question about Cookie De Voss. They're related—cousins who grew up together and met the De Voss men they later married."

"How can that be?"

"According to the background I dug up from the police archives, they were all sent to the same private boarding school in Santa Barbara. Well off, financially, they were still four kids from the hinterlands without social ties to anyone in the Santa Barbara area. The four became friends. Constance and Daniel married not long after graduating from high school. Ted and Bernadette went their separate ways for a few years. In fact, Ted was married for a short time to someone else. When Constance went missing, and Daniel died, it brought Ted and Bernadette together again. They married a few months later."

"What a sad story that is. It's too bad they didn't get their happily ever after once they married, even if their reunion was brought about by an awful tragedy. She didn't speak fondly of her husband or his family. From her rant today, I gather the police never solved the mystery of Constance De Voss's disappearance."

"That seems to be the case. In addition to reading what's in the written record about Daniel's death and Cookie's disappearance, I talked to a retired cop, Larry O'Reilly, who joined the force near the end of the investigation into her whereabouts. The County Sheriff's

Department was a small unit back then without much training or support from forensics. He recalls that they'd had very few leads and they went nowhere. The entire De Voss family was considered flakey—especially Cookie and Daniel who'd become involved in the drug culture and occult practices. Daniel wasn't just a drug user, but a would-be guru who proclaimed the benefits of mind-altering substances."

"Like Timothy Leary," I said.

"Yes, although when it comes to a member of the De Voss clan, apparently it's never easy to rule out money as the real motive behind anything they do."

"Are you saying Daniel De Voss was dealing in drugs?"

"That's what my old friend, Larry, heard. In keeping with the family rum-running tradition, Daniel De Voss was rumored to be smuggling in drugs from Mexico. Once the man was dead, no one pursued the matter further, so the rumors weren't ever confirmed or denied."

"Bernie De Voss may want to blame the police for the case going cold, but I can't imagine the De Voss family members were much help."

"They weren't. In fact, they did all they could to get Daniel's death ruled an accidental overdose and suggested that Cookie De Voss had taken off to join some cult. There was gossip, though, that she and her husband weren't getting along. One story about what happened was she asked for a divorce, Daniel killed her, and then committed suicide."

"Since no one ever heard from her again, that seems entirely possible, doesn't it? Even if she was done with her husband and his family, given how close she and Bernie De Voss were, it's surprising Cookie never contacted her if she was still alive."

"My thoughts, exactly. Although if she was fleeing from a domestic abuse situation, women are often advised not to contact anyone who's close to their spouse." Charly shrugged.

"I get it. It's like going into Witness Protection."

"Given the resources at their disposal, that might have been particularly good advice for anyone trying to evade the reach of the De Voss family. Cookie De Voss may not have even known that her husband died so soon after she was reported missing."

"Or maybe her husband wasn't the only member of the family causing Cookie problems."

"That wouldn't surprise me, either. Dottie was in the area at the time, and she remembers everyone being surprised when Daniel married Cookie instead of Bernie. It's too bad Bernie De Voss isn't willing to be more forthcoming. If she's having an affair with George Pierson, that's risky business. I'll bet Ted De Voss takes the 'til death do us part' marriage vow seriously."

When we reached the corner across from the Shakespeare Cottage, it was easy to see there was no police presence. I felt relieved, although we'd be safer once they arrived. As we stepped inside the front gate, Robyn dashed out onto the porch to greet us. There was a wild look in her eyes that made me feel bad for her.

"What's that?" I asked. Robyn looked at the smudges of white on her pants leg as she went back into the house and we followed her.

"It's ghost dust, I guess. I'm sure I brushed against him before I realized the great white heap on the floor in my pantry was Shakespeare's ghostly body." She responded with the wild look in her eyes growing wilder by the second. "The police are going to blame me, aren't they?"

"For what?" A voice said. We all turned to see Carl and Joe peering in from the porch.

"For killing Shakespeare's ghost since he's in my cottage and I'm the one who has complained endlessly about him."

"You can't be charged for killing a guy who's already been dead for a few hundred years. Besides, could you have murdered a ghost even if you wanted to do it?" Joe asked. Charly shook her head as she motioned for the two men to come inside.

"I heard the police let you go, but I was beginning to think you been taken into custody after all," I said. "Get in here and stand watch so no one else walks in the way you two did just now." They shut the door and turned on the porch light as the low light of dusk cast its long shadows everywhere. I took a long, hard look at Joe and Carl.

"Just so you're clear about what's going on, the police are on their way and ought to be here any minute now."

"Don't worry about them hauling us off. We didn't escape or do anything like that. Charly must have made a very strong case about our good character after Carl called her for help. Devers and this Vargas guy who stopped us in the first place turned us loose a few minutes later."

Charly raised an eyebrow as she made eye contact with me. We must have been thinking the same thing. I'm certain Hank had plenty to say about what characters they were. Poor Eddie Vargas must have already heard an earful from the deputy about his take on their "character" before Hank weighed in on the matter.

"It would have been nice of you to call and thank Charly for her help," I said.

"We'll do it now! Thanks for springing us before they could drag us in and really work us over. Putting up with Devers' threats was bad enough," Carl said.

"Yeah, it was nerve-wracking. Even if Hank only gives Darnell one bullet like Barney Fife, that's one too many. As soon as they said we could go, we took off before he could unholster the gun he was itching to use."

"Please don't tell me Deputy Devers is close enough that he's the one who's going to show up. Hurry, please." Robyn dashed down the hallway with Charly and me trying to catch up with her. I braced myself when Robyn stepped through the archway leading into the kitchen. There was no dead ghost lying on the floor.

"In here," Neely called. We moved toward the door to the pantry, and both dogs started whining and barking. Then I saw him. The body on the floor was dressed as we'd seen him a couple of nights ago. Costumed to resemble Shakespeare, he was covered from head-to-toe in a white substance. He looked ghoulish, but the blood pooled beneath him made it clear he was no ghost.

"Is it okay to put the dogs outside?" Robyn asked as they strained to get into the pantry.

"Sure," I replied rather absent-mindedly. "Domino was out there earlier today. She can show Emily around."

"There's no chance he's still alive, is there?" Charly asked.

"No. He's dead as a doornail." Neely stood over him and motioned for us to join her. "This is what I wanted you to see."

A note lay on the floor near the fingers on one hand. It was upside down, so we had to twist our necks to read the words. Written in a flowery script on a weathered piece of parchment paper, I read the words aloud as quickly as I could make them out.

"If a great wall could talk and gave up its secrets,
Even the darkest light would reveal the family vault
Then no one could deny the finder's right by default,
To keep its stolen treasures without regrets."

"Family vault. What family vault?" I asked.

"I don't know, but I guess that proves it, doesn't it?" Robyn asked from where she stood now that she'd rejoined us.

"Proves what?"

"That's no ghost lying on the floor. What would Shakespeare do with a treasure?"

12

Stony-Hearted Villains

"Eight yards of uneven ground is threescore and
ten miles afoot me, and the stony-hearted villains
know it well enough. A plague upon it when
thieves cannot be true to one another!"

—Henry IV

∞

"IS THERE A built-in safe in the cottage?"

"No one said anything about it when I moved in. If it's the De Voss family vault, there's no reason they'd want me to know about it, is there?"

"If George told Marty the truth, the family removed all their valuables before renting the cottage," Charly noted. "Maybe Shakespeare didn't get that update and believed the message he was toting around."

"What if this is related to the smuggling and they want to use the vault to store pricy items?" Charly shrugged. "Vault sounds sturdy, doesn't it? In my mind, that means it's much bigger than a wall-safe so there could be room to store smuggled loot. If it's about a hidden vault loaded with treasure, why has it taken so long to locate it?"

"The note is a little short on details about how to find the vault or open it if you do find it. Maybe those are the secrets the walls would give up if they could talk—a map to the vault and a key or code to unlock it." I nodded in agreement with Neely's suggestions.

"I wonder who wrote the note, don't you? The script and paper look old, but how old? Is it calligraphy, or is it written in someone's hand that Bernie or her husband might recognize?"

"Those are all good questions, Miriam. I hope Hank and his colleagues get cracking and try to answer them before there's more carnage. A break-in, a confrontation between two intruders, and an assault were bad enough. Now, two days later, the stony-hearted villains are at it again, and there's a dead body."

"If the villains who are responsible for the crime spree you're talking about are associated with the smuggling ring, this isn't the first murder to occur in connection with their operation. Maybe they've turned on each other. Hank must have some idea if that's happened."

"Or we're dealing with rival gangs of thieves. Shakespeare and the guy in the windbreaker didn't seem to be working together. What if there's more than one faction out to get to the vault and whatever is in it—or believed to be in it even if it's empty?" Neely asked.

"People have done worse to get their hands on a treasure that doesn't exist or an artifact like the Holy Grail that turns out to be a fake," Charly suggested. "Here's another question for you. How did Shakespeare get in here? I don't see a drop or streak of blood anywhere."

"Not through the front door that's for sure. The alarm

was still set when we arrived," Robyn explained. "I remember because I felt pressured to punch in the numbers that reveal it's me coming in through the door fast enough not to trigger a false alarm. If Shakespeare was able to do that, how did he get the new security code I just came up with yesterday?"

"Since he seemed to get in and out of the house as he pleased, maybe he'd figured out how to hack into the security system," Neely suggested.

"Can that be done?" I asked.

"Yes," Neely replied. "That's one of the things I researched the past couple of days trying to understand what's going on."

"Did Joe and Carl get back over here to reset the cameras?"

"I don't know," Neely responded.

"Neither do I," Robyn added. "Do you want me to go ask them?"

"That doesn't appear to be necessary," Charly said.

"The cavalry has arrived!" Joe called out as we heard stomping in the hallway. He and Carl led the way as Hank and Darnell followed. There was another man with them who I'd never seen before, but Carl and Joe knew him. They didn't seem all that chummy, so I guessed he was Eddie Vargas, the undercover cop they'd foiled earlier in the day.

The kitchen already felt crowded when representatives from the County Coroner's Office and the Forensics Unit also filed into the room. We stepped away from the pantry and moved to the center of the large kitchen.

"Let us get video documentation of the scene, okay?

Then you can have a quick look before we get to work."
The woman from the Coroner's Office, who'd taken
charge, eyed us suspiciously. As one of the forensic
investigators began snapping photos and recording video
of the body in the pantry, she spoke again.

"Which one of you called 911?" Robyn raised her
hand but didn't speak.

"She's the one who told the dispatcher she wanted to
report a murder, but then said she had Shakespeare's dead
ghost on her hands."

"I already told you that," Devers snapped.

"I was nervous," Robyn murmured. "Besides, you
haven't even looked at the guy yet."

"We would have been here sooner if the dispatcher
hadn't been concerned it was a crank call. It wasn't until a
second call came in that the police were notified and
informed us about the report of a body." Darnell shook
his head.

"She's been crying wolf for so long, no one takes her
seriously no matter what crime she reports." I heard
Robyn harrumph even though I was at the opposite end of
the lineup of people in the room. She put both hands on
her hips.

"Hey, Mr. Crime Scene Photographer, who's lying on
the floor in there?" Robyn suddenly cried out in a boom-
ing voice. The photographer turned around, abruptly.

"It's The Bard himself, and he's white as a ghost!"

"I rest my case." Robyn folded her arms over her chest.
Darnell opened his mouth to say something, but Hank
intervened.

"Drop it, Darnell. Enough, Robyn!" Hank was gruff.

His tone didn't change much when he directed his next question to the rest of us.

"Did one of you place the second call?" We all looked at each other and then shook our heads.

"It wasn't any of us, Hank. Did the second caller also report a murder?" I asked. It was their turn to stare at each other before a round of head shakes and shrugs. Darnell sniffed and cleared his throat to speak.

"That must be the case. When Vargas and I got the call, it was clear we were being sent to the scene of a murder. My only fear was that we were being put to the test once again by a group of tricksters with too much free time on their hands..."

"No one here cares about your fears. Save it for your therapy group." Then Charly turned to Neely. "Will you tell them exactly what happened when you and Robyn arrived half an hour ago?" Neely's statement was short and sweet.

"Why did you come back here tonight, Robyn? I thought you were staying with Neely Conrad for a few more days."

"I am, Detective. It's just that when Neely and I came here earlier, the property owner showed up. For some reason, Mrs. De Voss went off on us."

"What about?" Hank asked.

"She was riled up and ranted at Neely and me about eating at the dining table without putting the padding over the wood and asked me what I was doing here while the repairs were being done. I told her I still live here until my lease expires. I'm the one who's been inconvenienced, repeatedly, by uninvited guests. Restocking the pantry is on my dime, not theirs. If I didn't have the G.O.L.D. team on my side, I'd be facing this all alone and paying for a hotel room somewhere."

"G.O.L.D. team?" Vargas asked.

"It's not worth it, but I can explain," Darnell responded. "These *active adults* have overactive imaginations. One of their fantasies is that they're detectives—Grand Old Lady Detectives—if you can believe that." Neely spoke, abruptly, before Darnell could go on and on about an issue that he'd already said wasn't worth talking about in the first place.

"Robyn's understandably upset. Bernie De Voss stormed off and ordered us out. She insisted that the finishing work to be done was going to require the use of varnish or some sealers and she didn't want us to sue her for being exposed to the chemicals. We got out of here in such a rush that Robyn left her glasses behind, so we came back a few minutes ago to get them."

"Maybe, I should just pack up my stuff and leave, permanently. The way Mrs. De Voss spoke to me today, I'm not sure I should be renting from her anyway. Nor should anyone else, for that matter."

"Don't fret, Robyn. Miriam's got a few ideas about how you can do that if you're serious about moving out," Charly added. "Let's talk about it later." Robyn appeared relieved as Charly switched topics.

"From what Neely has said, Shakespeare must have been killed sometime during that last couple of hours, right?"

"That must be the case," I added although I couldn't be sure the question was meant for me. "Marty Monroe and I were having lunch with Robyn's landlord outside when we were also told to leave. We left at about three-thirty. Bernadette De Voss and George Pierson were still here. If you contact them, they can narrow down the window of time further."

"I can do that, now," a forensic investigator said. "Shakespeare's watch was smashed at five-nineteen. See?"

"That's a pricy broken watch," I said looking at the timepiece stashed in a clear, plastic evidence bag.

"You can say that again," Eddie Vargas added. "Ted De Voss has one just like it, and I heard he paid six figures for the one he wears." That sent a shock wave through me. It was, in part, sticker shock since when I'd said the watch was pricy, I hadn't realized that meant it cost over a hundred thousand dollars. On top of that, the prospect that the dead man was Ted De Voss and another member of the De Voss family had met with foul play made my head spin.

"Are you saying that's Ted De Voss lying there mas-querading as Shakespeare?" I managed to ask the question even though my voice sounded a little funny.

"No, no," Eddie Vargas replied. "Ted's an unusually tall man. Shakespeare looks to be of medium height. Besides, as the owner of the cottage, he could have searched this place at will without donning a disguise." What he said made sense. I nodded, trying to break the hold Eddie Vargas had claimed on me with a gaze that hadn't wavered as he answered my question. He'd spoken with a barely detectable accent, making me wonder about his role in the smuggling investigation. I broke the eye lock and asked another question.

"Did you pick up the note Shakespeare left?" All the lawmen in the room were peering at me. "As Neely told you, she checked to see if the guy was still alive. Otherwise, no one touched or moved a thing, but we couldn't help but notice the note lying next to him."

"I've got it." The crime scene investigator who'd shown us the broken watch held out a new evidence bag for Hank and the others to examine. "See? Poetic, huh?"

"Do you recognize the script, Vargas?" The intriguing undercover cop, with jet black hair and eyes to match, smiled at me again.

"It's Vargas to Devers, but to you, Miriam, it's Eddie."

"Okay, Eddie. Nice to meet you," I held out my hand which he grasped, shook, and then hung onto a little longer than necessary. All eyes in the room were on us. I took my hand back and stuffed it in the pocket of the jacket I was wearing.

"To answer your question, I don't recognize the handwriting, but I wonder if it's even handwritten. Don't you have someone who can tell us how this was printed, and what ink or paper was used? Or should I send it to the lab in LA or to my colleagues in San Diego for analysis?" That answered one of my questions about Eddie Vargas. He wasn't from around here.

"Let's see what we can find out using the County crime lab facilities. Then, if you want to send it elsewhere to find out more, we'll do it," Hank assured him with what seemed to be a tinge of annoyance in his tone.

Whose investigation is this? I wondered. As if I'd asked that question aloud, Hank took charge.

"So, what have we got, Neve?" Hank asked the rep

from the Coroner's Office who now had a name.

"The male victim is covered in white makeup and powder, so I won't have all the details about his features, scrapes, or bruises until I get his body to the morgue and clean him up. He's wearing a wig, and beneath that, he has on a stocking cap. It's covering what appears to be thin, dark hair, with a receding hairline. The costume and makeup mask his features, but I think there's a distinctive scar on the side of his face near his left ear. It's old, but it might help you determine his identity."

"Does that mean there's no wallet on the body?"

"Not that I can find, Hank. As I said, the victim is wearing multiple layers of clothing. Once we remove the Shakespeare disguise and take a better look at the clothing underneath, maybe we'll find identification secreted on him somewhere."

"What's the reason for all the blood?" Eddie Vargas asked.

"Someone stabbed him—or tried to stab him—several times. He has shallow cuts on his hands and arms, indicating he fought with his attacker. That may be how the watch was smashed, too, although that could have happened when he landed on the tile floor in the pantry. I can't say for certain, but I believe he was stabbed in the chest, and the weapon punctured his lung. The most likely cause of death is blood loss."

"If he put up a fight, why isn't there evidence of it in the pantry?" I asked.

"That's an excellent question. I believe the stabbing took place elsewhere. He managed to get away, but the damage had already been done."

"How far could he have gone with a punctured lung and bleeding the way he was? Wouldn't there be a blood trail coming from wherever the stabbing occurred?" Charly asked.

"That's what the crime lab investigators are here to discover. He certainly could have made it this far from the back yard or the garage, and all those layers of clothing could have absorbed most of the blood."

"You know this isn't the first time he's been here. He's sure been persistent, hasn't he?" That wasn't a completely idle thought because it was related to several other questions bouncing around in my head. "If he was a thief, why not just move on and pick an easier target?"

"That note says it all, doesn't it?" Joe asked. "The prospect of locating a vault full of loot must be what has kept him coming back." Devers appeared to be ready to issue one of his "butt out" decrees. Then Eddie Vargas responded.

"You could be right. Especially if the disguised man isn't just a thief, but someone who has caught treasure hunting fever. I've seen it happen before."

"I know what you mean! Like Humphrey Bogart hunting for gold in *The Treasure of the Sierra Madre* or those crooks in *The Maltese Falcon*," Joe suggested. "They weren't ever going to give up searching for it."

"Treasure hunting sure would explain why Shakespeare, the guy in the windbreaker, and who knows who else has been searching this place." Robyn paused. "Maybe if I'd known, I would have been doing that, too, instead of just straightening up after the greedy scoundrels for months."

"The search has gone on longer than that. My neighbor, Dottie Harris, who rented the Shakespeare Cottage before Robyn moved in, says she never saw a ghost. She did ask George if he, or someone he'd hired, had been in here. Like Robyn, Dottie noticed drawers ajar and items out of place."

"Did she get the same response from George?" I asked.

"Yes. Although George never mentioned the ghost, Rosemary Pfeiffer mentioned it to Dottie."

"Rosemary Pfeiffer is the receptionist in our community clubhouse if you want to speak to her," I said for the benefit of the police officials in the room. Charly picked up where she'd left off.

"Unlike Robyn, Dottie was only in the cottage for a few months. These treasure hunters must be more easily distracted than the ruthless rivals in pursuit of the Maltese Falcon. Their interest seems to wax and wane. Even Robyn wasn't constantly being harassed. Not until recently, anyway."

"It's impossible to believe this has gone on as long as you claim," Devers blustered. "They would have been caught long ago if it were true."

"That's if the people who could have caught them had done more to do so," Charly snapped. "I don't just mean the police, but the homeowners and the landlord. A comedy of errors, I guess."

"The note is cryptic. Anyone trying to find the vault or more clues to its location would have needed to search every wall in every room of the house," Hank suggested.

"He's done way more than that, as you could tell by the way he left the pantry after his last visit. If whoever's been in here has been looking for a vault, from what Robyn's told us, they've already checked for one hidden in a wall, behind the furniture, bookshelves, or pictures hanging on the walls," Charly pointed out.

"No one was in here last night," Joe stated with authority.

"How do you know that?" Devers asked with the pupils in his eyes narrowing to tiny pinprick sized openings.

"Don't get all worked up, Devers," Carl chided him. "We weren't out prowling around. We checked the feed from nanny cams we set up. There was no one on it."

"How difficult is it to check the video feed?"

"Not too hard. When no motion sets it off, the camera doesn't even record."

"We found nothing when we checked this morning, but grew concerned later that we'd screwed up when we installed the cameras. We came back here intending to check them again. Miriam warned us off because Bernie De Voss was still here, and she'd been on a rant. Then, we got sidetracked…" Joe shut up when Devers folded his arms. I'm sure Darnell had plenty to say about the trouble they'd caused after that.

"Show us where the cameras are set up in here, okay? Is the video stored in the cloud or on a memory card?"

"Both," Joe and Carl responded in tandem. "We'll give you SD cards, if you want them, or we can text you the information about how to check our cloud storage," Joe added.

"If we leave the SD cards in the cameras, we can continue to record if anyone else decides to visit the cottage." Hank nodded.

"Okay, leave them in place, and send me the information about how to access the cloud storage." Joe had slipped behind us, and pulled a barstool over to the cabinets above the stove. I couldn't believe my eyes as he scrambled onto the barstool and then moved some vines hanging from a silk potted plant on top of the cabinetry.

"Oh, yeah. This thing is working." In his excitement, Joe whipped his head around and gave us a thumbs up. The barstool wobbled, and so did he. Several of us ran to steady the chair and reached up to keep him from falling.

"Isn't one dead body enough for us to deal with today?" Charly scolded him as he slid off the barstool and onto the floor.

"You might not have been the only one lying dead on the floor, Joe," Robyn exclaimed, still a little breathless. "I could have had a heart attack!"

"Don't waste your breath. That guy can't learn," Darnell snapped. I wanted to come up with a clever retort, but to be honest, Joe's stunt had used up the last surge of adrenalin I could muster for the day.

"Hank, do you need us to do anything else, or are we free to go?"

"You can all go. Call me if you get to the video footage from today and find anything worth mentioning."

Nabbed! I thought. That was one of the main reasons I wanted to get out of here. Hank smirked as if he knew exactly what I was thinking.

"If you get done in the next couple of hours, feel free to drop by the Brontë Cottage for dessert. If we have anything new for you, we'll pass it on. Besides, Miriam needs to settle an old debt." All the eyes in the room were on me.

"Cookies," I said nervously. "It's a cookie debt..." Puzzled expressions were replaced by blank stares. "Never mind."

I was so flustered that I took a step toward the archway leading out of the kitchen before I remembered that Charly and I needed to retrieve Domino and Emily.

"The dogs sure have been awfully quiet, haven't they?" I asked. Our entire group moved to the sliders. When I flipped the lock and slid the sliding door open, I heard Neve speak.

"Did you catch that, Sabina?" Sabina was obviously the name of the female crime scene investigator.

"Yep. The door leading to the back yard will have prints on it we need to rule out."

"Mine are already on file," I hollered as I stepped out into the yard. Domino and Emily were nowhere in sight!

13

Unkindest Cut

"This was the most unkindest cut of all."
—Julius Caesar

∞

"**D**OMINO!" I SHOUTED. "Treats!"

"Where are they?" I asked as I checked to make sure the gate leading from the back yard to the street was still locked. I'd lied to myself when I'd said I was out of adrenalin. It was coursing through my body now, the blood too. It was pounding in my ears so loudly I could hardly hear my own thoughts. Had the bloodthirsty person who killed Shakespeare been lurking nearby and killed or taken the dogs?

"Over here!" Neely shouted from behind a pool house near the white privacy fence encircling the cottage property. I'd noticed the beautiful pool when we were here for lunch, but I'd been too distracted to pay more attention than that to the yard. Behind the structure, slats of the white fence lay on the ground.

Without giving it another thought, I slipped through the fence and onto the greenspace that merges with the golf course. About a hundred yards away, I spotted Domino and Emily. They were both digging as if they were having the time of their lives. I didn't like the fact that the spot in which they were digging had been cordoned off by a low fence of bright orange webbing.

"Domino! Emily! Come!" I commanded. When I looked back over my shoulder, I could no longer see the opening in the fence. A stand of trees blocked my view. If someone was sneaking on and off the property, that would be a way to do it. Why hadn't Cookie and Domino gotten out when we were having lunch with George Pierson earlier today?

"Charly," I shouted. "I've found them!" As I said that, the two rascals came running up to me. They weren't the least bit dismayed when I scolded them for leaving the back yard.

"What have you been up to?" I asked. That was a stupid question since Domino and Emily were covered in dirt. I took a stick Domino had in her mouth and tossed it away. Domino took off and retrieved it as if she were playing fetch. Charly and I both reached for it to take it away from her again, but she turned away.

"Oh, let her keep it," Neely said. "When you get home, you can get rid of it."

"Where's Robyn?" I asked.

"She went inside to confess that she could have been wrong when she thought Shakespeare had passed through walls to get into the house. Now she figures he just slipped in and out through the fence the way you did, and then let himself in with a stolen key. She wants to make sure Sabina checks out this spot."

"Didn't they inspect the grounds a couple of days ago after the break-in?"

"You'd think so. Robyn says she's never noticed there was a problem with the fence as long as she's lived here, or she would have said something about it."

"I'll bet it wasn't noticeable until our dogs made the escape route more apparent. I'd recognize Emily's teeth marks anywhere. It must have been held together with the ties lying around on the ground. They look well-chewed to me."

"Oh, great! We're in for a lecture about letting doggy spit contaminate the escape route," I sighed.

"No, you're not. Go on around to the front of the house from here. I'll cover for you while you and your canine culprits make your getaway."

"Thanks, Neely. I'm sure if they have questions for us, or the dogs, they'll know how to find us. I've just about had it with the law for one day."

"Does that include Eddie Vargas with the whitest, brightest, 'you can call me Eddie' smile anyone's ever seen?" Neely asked.

"Stop it," I said.

"Yeah, stop it, Neely. You know Miriam prefers men with piercing blue eyes." Charly smirked as Neely snorted.

"Detective Blue Eyes wasn't too happy with his pal cutting in on him, that's for sure," Neely said.

"He wasn't?" I asked. *Where was I?* I wondered. Eddie Vargas did have a dazzling smile, smoldering black eyes, and a nice wave in his thick black hair.

"If looks could kill, my dear, Neve would be hauling Vargas's body off to the morgue along with our Shakespeare impersonator who took a dagger to the chest."

"The 'unkindest cut of all,' to quote The Bard once more before you two leave his favorite haunt of late." Neely paused as if she heard someone coming and then spoke in a hushed tone. "If I had to take a stab at what was going on in Neve's mind by the way she was ogling him, I'd guess she'd prefer hauling Eddie Vargas back to the morgue alive." Then she and Charly both chortled. I was speechless listening to them carry on like that. They were still whooping it up when I heard Neve squawking.

"Speak of the devil," I muttered. Then I heard Deputy Devers' all too familiar bark.

"Now that's the perfect couple. Those two deserve each other," Neely added.

"Time to go before the posse corners us," I said.

"Good idea. I've got to order pizza. You need to go home and get those cookies for Handsome Hank." They giggled. I blushed. The dogs woofed.

"I hear those dogs! Where are they?" Devers asked, his voice louder now. Charly and I ran for it.

"They went that-a-way, Deputy. Or was it that way?" Neely chuckled as we bolted for home. I have no idea which way she told them we'd gone, but no one caught up with us or showed up at my door once Domino and I got home.

Less than an hour later, Domino and I were at the Brontë Cottage. Domino was outdoors again. She and Emily were playing a game with that old stick Domino had refused to give up. It had disappeared as soon as we got home, and then magically reappeared when we were leaving for Charly's house. Minutes after we got there, the pizza arrived, and so did our fellow snoops.

"I'm sorry Neve gave you a hard time," Midge said when she'd heard us griping about her. "If you'd called me, I would have come on over to Shakespeare Cottage. Neve is good at what she does, although she has an edge, but who doesn't? She's participated in training sessions I've run for medical staff who need continuing education credit, and we get along just fine. I'll call her tomorrow and get a copy of her preliminary report. Maybe, by then, she'll have learned something that can help us get this trouble resolved."

"You guys should have called us both. I would have loved to see that note you found. From the way Neely described him, Eddie Vargas sounds like a dish, too. I'm sorry I missed my chance to meet him."

"He looks pretty good," Joe said. "I used to look a lot like him when my hair was still dark."

"And when you still had most of it," Carl added.

"Joe has lots of hair, and there's hardly any gray in it. Although he gave all of us a few more with his floor show," Robyn said.

"Floor show is right—another few seconds this way or that, and that's exactly where he would have ended up—on the floor." Carl explained exactly what had happened.

"You guys have both had too many close calls during the past couple of days," Charly reminded them. "Given how fast the trouble has escalated, I'd say we all need to cool it. We'll let the police comb through all the evidence they've collected and try to figure out who killed Shakespeare's ghost. I'm not sure why Eddie Vargas is up to his neck in this since he's working with Hank on the smuggling investigation."

"From what he said, I gather he's with the San Diego Police Department or the County Sheriff's Department. I'll bet he's fluent in Spanish, given his surname and the hint of an accent."

"He is. I checked when I got home. He's part of a Special Operations Unit attached to the Sheriff's Department, and he's on a Task Force charged with improving Border Protection and Drug Interdiction. I don't get why he was at the cottage if he's supposed to be undercover."

"I wondered about that, too. What if the guy he was trying to hook up with saw him going in or out of there with the police?"

"That's sharp, Hemingway. What was he doing there in broad daylight after we got accused of risking the whole operation?" Joe asked.

"Maybe he gave up. He sure seems knowledgeable about Ted De Voss—calls him Ted and knows his watch when he sees it."

"If he's been charged with keeping Ted De Voss under surveillance, Eddie Vargas may know more about him than his wife does. Mickey Paulson is the name of the lowlife in the warmup suit, by the way. He's got a history of theft, drug possession, possession of stolen merchandise, assault—the list goes on and on. The guy spent seven years in prison for the assault charge, and he's obviously not on the 'windy side of the law.' I wouldn't put smuggling, burglary, assault, or even murder past him. What he's up to might get clearer once we know the identity of the dead man."

"When I call Neve tomorrow, I'll get the scoop about

who had the audacity to prowl around dressed like that. The Bard of Avon must be rolling over in his grave."

"He can rest easier now that the audacious dude prowls no more," Joe added. "At least you're not going to be involved in whatever's going on much longer, Robyn, so you can rest easier now, too."

"It's about time," Marty said. "You've already put up with enough not to have to be chewed out by an out-of-control landlady or that know-it-all woman from the Coroner's Office who spends most of her time with dead people."

"I can't believe I have a chance to buy the Du Maurier Cottage. It's like a dream come true." Robyn was smiling, despite the dire aspects of our discussion.

"Sometimes things work out just right, don't they? Now that you've got an offer on your condo, you can get the ball rolling on the purchase of your dream cottage. Both deals ought to close at about the same time," I said.

"Close enough!" Robyn exclaimed. "Even if the timing's a little off, that's okay. My realtor is taking backup offers on the condo so someone will buy it. It'll be wonderful not to wake up in the middle of the night to find some creep in my hallway. It was scary when I thought I was being haunted by the ghost of a literary legend. Now it's almost worse to know a real guy—with people trying to kill him—was roaming around just outside my bedroom door."

"Hank's on it, now. That's more good luck for you." Then Neely turned to Charly.

"It's odd that Mickey Paulson was back on the street driving by the cottage so soon after I broke his nose and only hours before Shakespeare was murdered. Now that you've told us more about his background, he goes to the top of my list of suspects."

"Mickey Paulson strikes me as the kind of a guy who couldn't resist cutting in on a treasure hunt if he got wind of it. So much of all the trouble the police are investigating is connected to the De Voss family one way or another. Do you really think that is Ted De Voss's watch they found on Shakespeare's body?" Marty asked.

"I'm sure we're supposed to believe it is," Neely replied. "What if it's a red herring? A false clue planted on Shakespeare's body to link Ted De Voss with the murdered man—whoever our Shakespeare impersonator turns out to be?"

"You could be right. I can't imagine Ted De Voss just gave it to Shakespeare, can you?" Joe's question hung in the air before Neely tried to answer it.

"What if Shakespeare worked for Ted De Voss, and the thief stole it from him? Then Ted De Voss got wind of it and paid Mickey Paulson to get the watch back. For a few dollars more, I'll bet Mickey Paulson would have made sure Shakespeare never had a chance to pilfer anything again."

"If it was a hit, it wasn't a very good one. Ted De Voss would have told Shakespeare's assassin to remove the watch and return it to him."

"It's not a very believable 'false clue' either, though. The police will be as skeptical as we are," Joe argued. "I take that back. Devers might fall for it."

"Well, it's got to be reason enough for the police to bring in Ted De Voss for questioning. At the very least, that ought to make him squirm. Or maybe it could be used as leverage to dig even deeper into his business dealings, or whatever it is the police are already scrutinizing," Charly said. "I'm as dubious as you are, Joe, that Ted De Voss is responsible for Shakespeare's murder."

"I agree. I don't believe he's guilty of murder—not for this one, anyway." Charly looked at me quizzically. "I've been trying to understand Bernie De Voss's behavior. Maybe her cousin, Cookie De Voss, didn't run off, and Bernie knows she's dead. That's why she came unglued when I brought it up."

"Who's Cookie De Voss?" A trio of voices inquired. Charly gave a quick rundown to those in our group who hadn't already heard about the case of the missing cousin. Marty sort of picked up where I'd left off.

"Bernie was shaking with rage or fear when you asked about Cookie De Voss's disappearance. If Cousin Cookie was murdered are you saying Ted De Voss did it and that's why Bernie De Voss freaked out?"

"Yes. Remember the words Bernie uttered with such rage? 'My disturbed husband's disturbed ancestors.' If Ted De Voss killed Cookie, and that led Daniel to kill himself, she lost two of the most important people in her life in a matter of days." Charly was nodding in agreement.

"That's a lot of anger to carry around for decades. Maybe she finally snapped and decided to set him up— even if she had to commit a new murder to have one to pin on him."

"If she's that far out, it would explain why it's such a clumsy attempt to frame her husband. Given the way she acted today, she's not thinking straight. Bernie De Voss is also one of the few people who would have had easy access to her husband's watch," I argued.

"Why now? Why Shakespeare? Why leave the watch and note there—is that a fake too?"

"I don't know. I don't know. Maybe." I responded. "I wish we had better answers to your questions, Neely."

"Here's a possibility. If Bernie De Voss is fooling around with George Pierson, and Ted De Voss found out, she's living on borrowed time," Midge suggested.

"Bernie De Voss is no dummy," I said. "If she figured the handwriting was on the wall, then desperation rather than revenge could have driven her to act. She had to get rid of her husband somehow before she disappeared like her cousin."

"Well, it's too bad her desperate scheme included murder. That makes her just one more 'disturbed' De Voss family member in my book. It was unnecessary, too, since the authorities are already on to her husband." Marty looked disgusted. "Given that a couple of members of his smuggling ring have already turned up dead, murder or conspiracy to commit murder must also be among the crimes they're investigating."

"So, why leave a fake note that seems to suggest it's 'finders-keepers' for anyone who locates a family vault filled with treasures?" Robyn asked.

"The watch is a big score for your average burglar. If Bernie De Voss is setting up her husband, knocking off Shakespeare is even more plausible if Ted De Voss did it to stop the guy before he found and claimed the family fortune," Midge suggested.

"That's if you believe a 'finders-keepers' note would hold up in court. If Ted De Voss was tailing Shakespeare close enough to tell a hitman where to find him, why not wait until he finds the family vault, takes the loot, and then grab him?" Charly asked.

"If Shakespeare was at it for as long as we think he was, maybe Ted De Voss got sick of waiting for the guy to find it. Or, if Shakespeare stole his watch, it was the last straw..." Neely's voice trailed off. "I don't know, either."

"Here's where Bernie De Voss's scheme really runs off the rails for me. If we're supposed to believe Ted De Voss was behind Shakespeare's murder, why have the thief killed on the De Voss property? If Ted De Voss had ordered Mickey Paulson to kill Shakespeare, why wouldn't he have told him to take The Bard for a ride, remove the watch and the note, and then throw him off a bridge or a boat into Steinbeck Cove?" Charly asked.

"He wasn't assaulted in the cottage. Maybe the plan was to kill him elsewhere, but something went wrong, and Shakespeare got away." Charly rubbed her face with both hands hearing my feeble attempt at an explanation. How could a guy in a Shakespeare costume, with a punctured lung and bleeding as bad as he was, get away from anyone or go far without being noticed?

"Shakespeare was a slippery character, I'll give you that. If what you're saying is true, he got away twice assuming Mickey Paulson was in the cottage to abduct or kill Shakespeare before Neely fought with him. Let's see what Hank and his crew of investigators come up with. We need something concrete to sort out the possibilities that this is, 'A,' a ridiculous ploy by Bernie De Voss to get revenge on her husband; 'B,' the work of rival treasure hunters working at cross-purposes; 'C,' some conflict having to do with a smuggling operation; or 'D,' Ted De Voss loses it after a small-time thug steals his expensive watch and has him killed in the dumbest way ever. All of these options seem pretty far-fetched, but the picture's still awfully murky at this point."

"Well here's a murky picture to add into the mix," Carl said. He'd brought out his laptop after we finished eating, but he'd been so engrossed in the conversation that he hadn't reviewed the video from Shakespeare Cottage until now.

"Uh, the picture's not murky at all. It's what it means that's unclear," Joe commented as he watched the video footage with Carl. "Show them."

Carl turned around the laptop and played the video clip as we all leaned forward to watch it. In the empty kitchen of the Shakespeare Cottage, the door to the pantry suddenly opened. Then it swung wide, and Shakespeare hit the floor in the pantry.

"Is that all? How did he get in there? When?" Neely asked, spitting out rapid fire questions.

"Oh, come on. Something must be wrong. Play it again, please," Midge said. "Start at the last point where the camera recorded previous activity, okay?" Carl did as she asked. The last thing the camera recorded before Shakespeare opened the door to the pantry—from the inside—was George Pierson moving about. He checked the doors in the kitchen to make sure they were locked, switched off the lights, and then left the room.

"The hallway camera records him leaving through the front door at three-fifty-four. There's nothing on any of the cameras until Shakespeare opens the pantry and drops to the floor at five-twenty-four—minutes after the watch he was wearing had stopped."

"Well, folks, maybe I've seen too many old murder

mysteries. There's only one explanation for a treasure hunter who comes and goes at will, and pops up out of nowhere," Neely said, pausing for dramatic effect, "a secret passageway." My initial response was to scoff at the idea, and then I reconsidered.

"How about a network of narrow passageways? That would explain why the realtor gave Robyn a smaller estimate of the interior in the place she was going to rent compared to the larger footprint evident from outside."

"If there's an entrance in the hallway as well as the pantry, maybe Shakespeare could have appeared to pass through the walls as Robin has claimed all along. In a way, that's what he did," Marty said excitedly.

"We stood there, staring into that pantry today. Police investigators have been in there twice now. Robyn's kept that pantry stocked for over a year. If it's there, the entrance is well-hidden, but I can't come up with a better explanation for how he got in there."

"I'm not really talking anything like you might have found in the creepy old cursed Seaview Bluffs Manor house. Given the De Voss families' disreputable activities during Prohibition, they may have added a priest hole or a hidden trap door under a rug leading to the cellar. There's a whole new technology being used to build panic rooms nowadays. I've never researched it, but a builder must be able to equip panic rooms with escape routes. A fancier version of the tunnels Al Capone supposedly built under the Two Bunch Palms resort near Palm Springs to get away."

"I can just hear that buffoon, Devers, bellowing that this is the craziest idea we've come up with yet," Midge argued.

"Then, let's prove it. We'll show him rather than tell him. I'm still the legal tenant in the Shakespeare Cottage. Let's go find the entrance that's hidden at the back of the pantry." I gulped, not relishing the idea of doing that in the dark of night with a killer on the loose.

"Okay, Robyn, I agree," Charly said enthusiastically. "That's what we'll do the first thing tomorrow, assuming the police don't still have the place under wraps. We're still expecting a visit from Hank. If he's seen the video clip, he may already have a team in there, or on their way, to find out how Shakespeare got in there."

"Well, I wouldn't get too excited about the police acting quickly. Even if Hank, or someone else at the Sheriff's Department, has reviewed all the video footage, the authorities are more likely to believe we goofed up the recording somehow than to reach the conclusion that there's a hidden entrance to a secret passageway," Marty added.

"It is far-fetched. Unless Hank brings it up, I suggest we put off any discussion of the matter until we've had a chance to look around tomorrow," Carl argued. No one hesitated to agree.

"I need a cookie break," Joe said as he jumped to his feet. The rest of us stood and headed to the kitchen with him. I called Domino and Emily to come inside for a treat, too. When Domino sauntered into the house with Emily at her heels, she still had that stick in her mouth. She followed me into Charly's kitchen, and Midge gasped.

"I'm sorry. It's a dirty old stick, but Domino won't part with it."

"That's no stick, Miriam. That's a bone from a human forearm—part of one, anyway."

14

A Wise Father

"It is a wise father that knows his own child."
—The Merchant of Venice

∞

WE WERE ALL dumbfounded by Midge's assertion about Domino's new favorite toy. I was also completely grossed out wondering where it had been in my house. I hoped not in my bed, but I was going to change the sheets when I got home just in case.

Everyone was silent as I offered Domino a chunk of chicken to get her to drop the bone. It worked, but as you might expect from any good, suspenseful moment in a mystery, the doorbell rang. We all yelped. Domino wolfed down the chicken treat, picked up the bone, and ran to the front door with it. We all dashed down the hall after her.

"Come in, quickly, Hank," Charly said. "We're in the middle of a situation with Domino. Domino who stood there wagging her tail, suddenly decided to show Hank her bone the way she had done with me the first time I saw it. There was no trickery required. When Domino placed the bone at Hank's feet, he bent down and picked it up.

"Don't throw it! That could be evidence!" I shouted as I ran and plowed into Hank, almost bowling him over. He grabbed hold of me to steady himself, wrapping his arms around me, which wasn't all that bad except that we had an audience.

"Smooth, Hemingway," Joe said. "You should have saved that move for when you two were alone." He snickered, and he wasn't the only one who found it funny. I wanted to be annoyed by the teasing, but Hank had on some fragrance that was intoxicating. The big grin on his face made me feel loopy.

Somehow, I managed to take a step back. As Hank released me, he examined the bone he held. Domino was so sure the game was on, she woofed and wiggled, and did the little bowing thing she does when she wants to play fetch or another of her favorite games.

"Here, use this," Charly said and handed Hank a large dog chew. Hank tossed it down the hall, and both dogs flew after it. "Here's one for you, too, Emily." Charly sent a second treat skidding down the hallway as she handed me a large zip lock plastic bag. I unzipped it and glanced over my shoulder to make sure Domino was still busy.

"We ought to get it out of sight. It won't take Domino any time at all to figure out she's chasing a fake." Hank dropped the bone into the plastic bag which Charly then slid into a padded envelope.

"Where did she find it?" Hank asked, as I walked to the nearby powder room and washed my hands. I'd only touched it for a second before the doorbell rang and Domino snatched it back, but I felt like bugs were crawling up my arms. Hank followed my lead and scrubbed his hands.

"In what looked to me like a sinkhole or a trench that's been dug. It has that orange webbed fencing around it that's used to keep anyone from straying into it. Not that it stopped Domino and Emily."

"Is it on the golf course or the De Voss property?"

"It's outside the fencing around Shakespeare Cottage, although it's not too far away. Joe can probably tell you if that means it's on the golf course or the De Voss's private property."

"Let's go ask him," Hank said as he smiled at me again. "You look great, by the way." I sort of bumped into the doorway as I walked backward exiting the powder room.

"Thanks," I replied and quickly moved on. "My guess is Joe has returned to the kitchen for a cookie break. I'll fix you a plate of cookies if you haven't had dessert yet."

"Show me the way," he said, with the padded envelope tucked under one arm. The room was full of grinning people when we walked into the kitchen. Joe's cheeks bulged like a squirrel gathering acorns to store for winter.

"Joe, if you can spare a minute from your cookie binge, Hank has a question for you." He nodded, swallowed, and downed a big swig of milk.

"Sure, Hank. There's no need to ask though. Hemingway will be happy to go out to dinner with you. She sent me a note saying she really, really likes you." I gasped as the room erupted in laughter.

"Ghostbuster, barstool dancer, and matchmaker—is there no end to your hidden talents?" Robyn asked. She'd asked that question with apparent sincerity, but she had to be joking. Then she batted her eyes at Joe in an exaggerated, flirtatious fashion, and more laughter followed.

"You want me to pass him a note for you?" Carl asked raising both eyebrows.

"I wouldn't mind." Then she batted her eyes at Joe again. I laughed, too. The flummoxed expression on Joe's face was priceless.

"I'd say that clinches it. Robyn would be happy to go out for dinner with you, Joe." Carl's ruddy complexion was flushed with good humor.

"Hey, why not? I'll pop for a burger if you want to celebrate your new house." Talk about smooth! Right in front of all of us, he and Robyn had just arranged a first date. "What's your question, Hank?"

Joe scooted over and motioned for Hank to step closer to the bar area where we'd set out the food. I followed, grabbed a dessert plate, and handed it to Hank as he spoke to Joe.

"Do you know the spot out behind the De Voss property that's cordoned off?"

"Yeah, Miriam told us that's where Domino dug up her treasure today."

"Is it on the golf course or private property?"

"Technically, it's a large greenspace that belongs to the De Voss family. No one else can build in that area, so they'll always have privacy. Because it's not enclosed space or posted as private, residents and members of the public who come to play golf wander onto it. The managers of the golf course are charged with maintaining the area. That usually involves routine lawn care and maintenance, but something happened in that spot."

"Miriam said she thought it might be a sinkhole."

"It could be. The ground in that spot has shifted. The water to the sprinkler system has been shut off while the golf club management team tries to figure out how big a problem they have, and how deep the hole is. This is no DIY job. They've called in civil engineers to review the developers' plans from back in the sixties, find out what's caused the problem, and recommend a fix."

"Gosh, they ought to have George Pierson look at it given how much he knows about dirt," Marty muttered.

"How could Domino have found a human bone in there?" I wondered aloud. "It's not built on an old burial site or anything like that, is it?

"I've never heard we have sites like that up here on the high bluffs. Down below and closer to the beach in the preserve, yes. Besides, the bone must have been placed in the ground more recently than what's under it. When the ground sank, what was above it shifted, and filled in the hole ending up on top." I nodded at Joe's explanation which made perfectly good sense to me.

"Are you suggesting that a body buried nearby tumbled into the pit?" Marty asked.

"Yep."

"Then there must be more bones," I said.

"I'll call forensics and get them to send a team out there tomorrow." Hank put down the cookie he was eating, pulled out his phone, and made a note. "Will someone be able to show them to the spot?"

"Sure. If they stop at the gate, security will escort them to the spot. They'd better bring the County engineers with them, though, before they poke around too much," Carl warned. "Depending on how much dirt those dogs kicked up today, it could be even more unstable than it already was."

"Those hounds are lucky they didn't trigger a landslide while they were partying like wild animals," Joe added.

"Can someone from forensics figure out who was buried there with one bone?" Marty asked. "Or how long the body's been in the ground?"

"They can get DNA from the bone, but that won't help much unless the person's DNA is already in a database or on file somewhere," Midge replied. "They should be able to estimate how long it's been buried." Hank nodded.

"They can tell if it's a man or woman from the DNA, right?" Robyn asked.

"Yes."

"If it's a woman, maybe it's Cookie De Voss," Robyn added. Hank did a double-take.

"What do you know about Cookie De Voss?" he asked.

"Only what Miriam and Charly told me."

"Which wasn't much," I said, defensively. Even though Hank hadn't asked me anything, his eyes had settled on me after searching Charly first.

"It was enough for Bernie De Voss to get her knickers in a twist," Marty snapped. Hank put up both hands, signaling us to stop.

"Start at the beginning and tell me the whole story," Hank said as he stuffed a triple ginger snap into his mouth. He scarfed down one cookie after another as we filled him in on what Charly and I had learned about Constance De Voss and how Bernie De Voss had reacted to my question about her cousin who went missing so long ago.

"Okay, if it turns out to be a woman, I'll have forensics look for a comparison sample of DNA from the missing De Voss woman. Maybe they can find more skeletal remains, and that'll help determine the person's identity—if they can get the bones out of that pit without getting themselves killed." Hank stopped speaking, and I thought he might be about to leave. Instead, he loaded his plate with more cookies.

"I came here thinking I'd share a bit of news with you." We all went on alert. Hank shook his head. "It's impossible to keep ahead of the active adults in this room."

"Don't hold out on us," I implored him.

"Yeah, we know how to keep a secret." I glanced at Robyn before she could go on. Since he hadn't said a word about the video footage recorded at Shakespeare Cottage today, I didn't want her to let anything slip. Robyn zipped her lips.

"Please do keep this quiet. We've discovered the Shakespeare impersonator's identity. It'll hit the news in a day or so, but we've just notified the family, so we'd like to give them a chance to come to grips with what's happened."

"So, who is it?"

"Danny De Voss," Hank replied.

"You can't mean Ted De Voss's brother. He was already dead."

"Not his brother. His son." I was stunned as I went over what I'd learned about the De Voss family. I hadn't considered the prospect that Ted and Bernie De Voss had children. Any mention of their offspring would probably have shown up in more recent HOA history or events than the ones I'd reviewed. I wondered if Danny De Voss was as antagonistic toward his father as his mother seemed to be this afternoon.

"Were Ted and his son on good terms?" I asked.

"No. That wasn't news to us. Ted De Voss doesn't appear to have ever shown much interest in his son."

"Shakespeare had something to say about that," Midge offered. "'*It's a wise father that knows his own child.*'"

"I don't know how much Ted De Voss knows about his son. We learned early in our investigation you stumbled into by chasing Mickey Paulson, that father and son have been estranged for years. To turn Shakespeare's saying on its head, Danny De Voss may have been wise to his father's activities, but he doesn't appear to have become involved in them. Like his parents, he went away to boarding school in Santa Barbara and then went to college. He eventually got a degree after switching colleges several times—mostly because of lousy grades, but he also got into trouble for cheating on exams and public drunkenness."

"The cheating incident sounds like Danny was following in his father's footsteps, if your investigation proves that Ted De Voss is leading a smuggling ring."

"The jury's not in on that yet, but it won't be long before Ted De Voss has his day in court. We're close to making arrests in the case which is another reason not to talk about any of this to anyone."

"Danny De Voss must be in his late thirties or early forties by now. What did he do after he finished college if he didn't join the family business?" Charly asked.

"The family owns legit businesses, too. Danny De Voss runs a chain of restaurants the family launched decades ago. At the time, they were fronts for serving bootleg liquor in backrooms where they also sponsored illegal card games and betting. He seems to have done a credible job, but they're not hugely profitable."

"Did his father give him the watch or did he steal it?"

"I don't know yet, Carl. That's only one of the many questions we hope to answer. Given what you've told me about your interactions with Bernie De Voss today, I'm betting she'll be happy to help us if she believes her husband had anything to do with their son's death."

"If she lives long enough to do that," I commented.

15

The Greatest Sound

"But the saying is true: 'The empty vessel makes the greatest sound.'"
—Henry V

OUR GET-TOGETHER ENDED soon after Hank's revelation that the mysterious intruder masquerading as Shakespeare's ghost was Daniel De Voss. I'd walked out with Hank to give him the box of cookies I owed him. He'd taken the opportunity to point out that a dinner date wasn't a bad idea. I didn't argue with him and we settled on a time and place. Charly grinned from ear-to-ear when I told her. When Domino and I reached home, I still had butterflies in my stomach about it. It was nice to experience them from excitement about a pleasant event for a change.

When I woke up the next morning, I called Charly to tell her I was on my way. It was only seven-thirty. We'd agreed to get to Shakespeare Cottage early and search for a hidden passageway, hoping to stay ahead of whatever ripple effects there might be from yesterday's shocking events. Last night, Carl had spotted a headline that had already reached social media sites referring to *"The Murder of Shakespeare's Ghost."*

Even though Hank had succeeded in keeping the identity of the victim secret, it hadn't taken a crafty local newscaster long to find out that a murder had occurred in the Seaview Cottages community. That the incident had occurred at Shakespeare Cottage was easy enough to discover by intercepting the police dispatch after Robyn had called 911. How the reporter learned that the victim was disguised as Shakespeare's ghost wasn't clear to me or anyone else.

When Charly and I arrived at the Shakespeare Cottage, we went straight to the kitchen. I was shocked to find Neely already in the pantry and on her knees running her hands along the base at the back wall. Robyn was doing something similar but higher up. When Neely looked up at me bleary-eyed, she pushed her glasses up on her nose with one hand, and then gave us a little salute.

"Greetings," I said. "How can we help?" We'd left our doggie delinquents home alone today after their close call yesterday.

"Can you drag a ladder in here so we can reach higher?" Robyn asked. "I keep a stepladder in the laundry room. If you think we need a bigger ladder, I've seen one in the garage that I've never used."

"Let's start with the stepladder and if we can't reach as far as we need to, we'll get the larger one. Have you found any clues yet?"

"Possibly. Before we cleaned up, we noticed a streak of what looked like blood, here, close to the back wall. I'm sure the forensic investigators must have seen it, but they might not have given it a second thought. Considering its location in the context of searching for a hidden passage-way, I felt it might be a hint that Shakespeare left that streak as he entered the pantry from behind the wall."

"Neely took a photo with her cellphone, but that wasn't very helpful. We marked the spot with a felt tip pen, though. See?"

"Robyn insisted we clean up in here. It was disgust-ing—not the best sight to see at the crack of dawn."

"We couldn't work in here, that's for sure."

"Thanks for doing that, you two," I said. "I'll go get the stepladder." When I returned, Charly had joined the hunt. She was stretching as high as she could, running her hands over the wall adjacent to the back wall on the left. Most of it was lined with shelves. The area she searched held a pegboard with hooks. She was examining each hook to see if it moved, like a lever that might trigger a door to open if she wiggled it.

I handed the stepladder to Robyn who took it from me. I was about to offer to climb up on the ladder when I heard footsteps and voices.

"Good morning!" Joe bellowed when he and Carl came into the kitchen. Midge and Marty were right behind them.

"Any luck?" Marty asked.

"We've only been at it a few minutes," Charly re-sponded. "Neely and Robyn got here ahead of us and cleaned up enough so we could stand to work in here."

"It's already crowded. If you need us to help in there, we can, but I thought Carl and I could check the hallway for any sign of an entrance since Shakespeare turned up there so often."

"That's a great idea!" Robyn exclaimed.

"What's on the opposite side of this wall in the garage?" Midge asked.

"I'm not sure. There are shelves lining it, but I don't know how they sync up with the location of the pantry."

"Then Marty and I will go try to figure that out while you finish searching in here."

"Do you have any reason to believe we're not nuts?" Marty asked. Robyn told them about the blood streak they'd cleaned up before we arrived and pointed to the 'x' she'd used to mark its location.

"Hmm, that's not much, but it is a little odd given where the body was when you found it."

"Have you tried knocking on the walls? If there's an opening or an empty passage behind the wall, it ought to sound different when you locate it. Have you heard the old saying *an empty vessel makes the greatest sound*?'" Midge asked.

"It's vaguely familiar," I replied.

"I've heard it before. Is it another famous saying from Shakespeare?" Robyn asked.

"He used it, but he didn't coin the phrase. It was an old proverb already in use when he was around."

"Let's give it a try," I said.

"Knock, knock. Anybody home?" I called out as I began knocking on the wall from right to left.

"Wait! I want to do that again!" Neely said. She repeated the knock-knocks I'd used, starting from the left side and moving toward the center this time. "Well, I'll be a son of a gun!"

"Something's different here toward the middle. Let's keep at it!" I said, starting over again higher up on the wall.

"Carl and I are going to go play 'knock-knock' in the hallway."

"We'll check out the garage." Our group dispersed and for the next hour, we scoured every inch of the pantry. The knock-knock strategy had revealed what could be an opening large enough for Shakespeare to pass through, but we had no success in finding any sign of a mechanism to open it.

"What should we do?" I asked.

"Maybe it's time to get a sledgehammer," Neely suggested.

"They'll sue me!" Robyn cried.

"Don't worry. We won't do that. Hank might arrest us for vandalism or obstruction of justice or something." I was frustrated and leaned against the wall, listening.

"Let's keep knocking, okay? I'm sure I woke up more than once because I thought I heard someone knocking at the door. There wasn't anyone there, of course, so I just added 'hearing things' to the list of symptoms I planned to report when I finally agreed with Devers that I needed my head examined." I nodded.

"Yoo-hoo! Anybody in there?" I asked before I started again.

"Will you stop asking that question? Do you really want someone to answer and invite you in?" Neely suddenly gasped, as I knock-knock-knocked on the door three times. The wall appeared to sink and then slid open.

"Yippee!" I hollered. Robyn and Neely shouted, too. "Joe! Carl!" I yelled. Charly dashed to the door that led from the kitchen to the garage just as Marty and Midge opened it and came inside.

"We heard shouting! Is everything okay?" Marty's eyes widened as she spotted the gaping opening in the wall. "There's no light in there, huh?"

"I'll check," Joe said as he raced to the opening. He didn't go far before he grunted. He stepped back into the pantry rubbing his nose. "It's not very roomy in there. Do you have a flashlight, Robyn?"

"Lots of them," she replied. In seconds, she'd gone to a drawer in the kitchen and came back with not one, but two flashlights. "I never wanted to get caught in the dark in this house with you-know-who on the loose. There are more flashlights stashed in the laundry room's storage cabinet. There must be almost enough for each of us to have one."

"I'll be back in a minute." I ran to get them. The idea of being stuck in a narrow passageway in the dark didn't appeal to me even though we no longer needed to worry about bumping into Shakespeare's ghost in there. When I reached the laundry room, I suddenly wondered if there was a passageway in here, too. A few triple knocks later, a panel in the wall did the sink and slide thing again. This opening was closer to Robyn's master suite. Maybe she'd heard knocking when Shakespeare used this doorway.

I leaned forward, and without stepping into the passageway, I bathed the corridor in a beam of light. It was narrow and ran in both directions. I was about to pull my head out of the opening when, off to my right, I glimpsed what appeared to be stairs leading down into the darkness. Laughter drew my eyes to my left. In the distance, I could see a dim glow which had to be coming from the opening in the pantry.

On impulse, I stepped into the passageway and took a couple of steps toward the source of that light. The opening behind me slid closed. I felt panicky, turned around, and knocked three times. Nothing happened. I tried it again. Still nothing. Then I switched to two knocks and a single knock without success. Panic hit me again, and I bolted toward the light hoping I'd reach it before Joe or someone else stepped into the passageway, and that doorway closed too. I was afraid to call out for fear that would cause someone to bolt into the passageway and trigger the door to close.

"We've got a problem," I said as I stepped back inside the pantry and the door slid shut behind me. When the screaming died down, I explained what I'd done and told them about the stairs I'd seen before I locked myself out of the house, so-to-speak.

"You must have tripped an infrared photosensor or something—you know like the automatic sensor that keeps your garage door from closing if there's something in the way. I'm lucky I turned back around after banging my head against the wall without moving right or left before I came back in here."

"Do you want to try it again?" I asked. Joe considered it as I knocked three times and the door opened again.

"Will one of you do the triple knock from inside and let me back in if I can't figure out how to get it to open? I've got a touch of claustrophobia." Carl's lips twitched, and then he nodded yes.

"Of course, we will," he replied with a serious tone in his voice. His upper lip quivered again, though.

"Not you, pal. You're going with me. I don't trust you."

"Good grief! Let's try this to test your idea, although that must be why the door shut after Miriam moved around in the passageway." Robyn reached up and took down a long metal tool from a hook on the pegboard. "This is my grabber I use to get things off the upper shelves without dragging the step stool in here."

Without another word, Robyn put one foot into the passageway then swished the grabber around on one side and then the other. The door began to shut, slowly, as she stepped back into the pantry. I used the triple knocks again, although this time, I made much less noise. The entrance to the passageway opened again anyway.

"I guess it's not about the volume," I said.

"Vibrations, maybe," Charly suggested. "The rhythm or a counter of some kind because the number of knocks matters."

"Now that we know it'll open again right away, let us try a few things," Joe said as he motioned for Carl to join him. Once they were in the passageway, Joe tripped the beam and the door slid shut. "If we're not back in five…"

The panel must be soundproofed because I didn't hear another word as soon as it shut. We milled about, nervously, as I kept my eye on the minutes ticking by. I was about to use the triple-knock trick we'd learned to open the door when it moved on its own.

"Shave and haircut," Joe said in a sing-song voice. Carl

responded quickly.

"Two bits." Then they both stepped back into the room and explained the knocks they tried, including the Morse code S.O.S. signal before they found the one that worked.

"That's from a really old song, but I knew guys in Vietnam who used it to figure out if a new POW in the next cell was from the U.S."

"Now what?" Carl asked.

"I want to go see where those stairs lead."

"I wondered why no one ever reported seeing Shakespeare coming and going above ground until we chased him down that night. There must be another way in and out of here that's underground."

"Do you think it's possible to block this open just in case our knock-knock code doesn't work?" Marty asked in an anxious tone.

"Why don't we try that before we go any further?" I took the stepladder, opened it, and set it in the way to prevent the door from shutting. Then Robyn used her grabber to trigger the door to close. That worked! It might be a little tricky for one of us to squeeze through or crawl under the ladder, but it was good to have a backup plan if we couldn't get the code to open the door here or at the laundry room's entry point.

I handed out the flashlights and stepped into the passageway first. The others followed and their beams bounced around striking the walls, ceiling, and floor. The floor beneath us was tile. The walls were made of dark wood that sometimes seemed shiny and reflected the light. In other places, it was as if the walls absorbed the light. I wondered if anyone else had noticed or had an explanation, but I was more motivated to see where those stairs led.

The stairs were narrow, stone steps that abutted cinder block walls on both sides. Our house in Ohio had a basement with walls that looked very similar. This one had been dug deep—I counted eighteen steps before we reached a floor made of poured cement. I stepped away from the stairs and the open space widened.

"Wow!" Joe said as he joined me. "Will you look at this?"

16

Neither Rhyme nor Reason

"Was there ever any man thus beaten out of season, when the why and the wherefore there is neither rhyme nor reason?"
—The Comedy of Errors

∞

A CORRIDOR STRETCHED out ahead of us. It was wide enough that I could stretch out both arms without touching the walls. In fact, it was large enough you could drive a golf cart down here. I'm not sure why that idea popped into my mind since there wasn't any obvious way to get anything that large down here. Then, off in a corner, my flashlight caught a forklift in its beam. Clearly, there was an entrance somewhere that had been used to get that down here.

What had caused Joe to express such amazement was the fact that the main corridor went on as far as we could see in the beams of our flashlights. More than that, though, it appeared as if there was a network of passageways leading off to the left from the main corridor. As my eyes adjusted to the dim light, I could see doorways on our left and right.

"What the heck is this place?" Midge asked. "For me, *'there is neither rhyme nor reason'* for an underground complex that's so, so...complex."

"I thought if we found a secret passageway, it might be part of an escape route for De Voss family members to use if they were under siege—by police or by bad guys. Now, I'm not so sure." Charly paused sweeping the area, bathing it in light. "It doesn't make rhyme or reason to me, either."

"Especially since De Voss family members no longer live here," Robyn added.

"This must have been built back when the cottage was constructed more than fifty years ago. We're under their garage or the back yard. I'll bet there's an entrance in the garage and maybe one in the pool house, too," Charly asserted. Neely walked over to a nearby metal door.

"Is it the vault?" Joe asked. "Have we found the hidden family treasure?"

"It's no vault and it isn't that well-hidden or Shakespeare would have found it long before he was murdered," Neely said. "Besides we're not here on a treasure hunt." As soon as Neely opened the door, overhead lights flickered on.

"This is heavy and solid enough to take a bullet," Neely said as she opened a door which looked a lot like those in restaurant kitchens. "Someone sure was paranoid."

"Now this is a pantry where I could be prepared for any disaster!" Robyn exclaimed as we filed into the room. The large room was lined with shelves piled high with food, toiletries, and other supplies. "I'll admit to being on the paranoid side when it comes to apocalyptic events. The steel doors are great, too."

"It's not paranoia if people really are after you," Joe noted.

"That's a good point. By the sixties when the cottage was built, at least three generations of the De Voss family had been involved in dangerous, illicit activities, and some had paid for it with their lives."

As Charly said that, first aid supplies caught my eye. In addition to food and bottled water, there were batteries, lanterns, blankets, tools, soap, and toilet paper. All sorts of other items were stacked in here, too, including paintings and old lampshades, throw pillows, and other things like that. Neely, who was peeking over my shoulder at the odd assortment, pointed to a painting that had been propped up alongside a couple of others.

"Those are interesting. Someone was a fan of Tolkien—see? That's Gandalf, those are hobbit huts, and the tower with the wall around it must be the Tower of Isengard. Not the family fortune, but they're more interesting than the other stuff in here."

"I agree. It's also interesting how much is stowed away in here. Someone laid in enough supplies that you could live underground for months. Maybe it was built to serve as a fallout shelter. Paranoia about a nuclear attack was rampant around the time the cottage was built in the sixties."

"If that was the main purpose, I doubt anyone would have gotten rid of the old supplies and replaced them with the newer ones that are in here. I make sure I do that with my disaster preparedness rations—especially the food. It's dusty in here and you can tell someone's visited recently." Robyn commented as she pointed to places where items had been moved leaving voids in the dust on some of the shelves. "Maybe Shakespeare was living down here since he was such a frequent visitor these past few months."

"You could be right about that," Charly responded as she left the room and walked over to another door across the way that was made of heavy metal. There was a keypad alongside it, but there was no light indicating that it was activated. In fact, up close, it appeared as if it had been pulled loose from the wall. In any case, the door swung open when Charly gave the handle a yank. "Wow—this is what I call a panic room!"

We all walked into a well-lit, tiled foyer. The lighting in here was more like daylight than that rendered by the fluorescent overhead lighting in the storage room. It's as if we'd walked into a hotel suite circa 1970. No windows, of course, but the living room with orange and brown shag carpet was as comfortable as any you'd find above ground. A dining area, kitchen, along with several bed-rooms and bathrooms could have provided enough room for the whole De Voss family. Close quarters, though, if you weren't on good terms which seemed to be the case for Bernie, Danny, and Ted.

"What a hideout," I said aloud. "Perfect if you have to lock yourself up. It's a gorgeous jail cell."

"It sure beats going to a real one," Joe quipped.

"Or ending up in a tomb which this place also calls to mind," Charly added.

"Someone's been sitting in my chair," Joe said in a

gruff voice that probably was supposed to be Papa Bear. "Guess who?" There were white streaks on the edge of one of the large club chairs near us. Shakespeare's ghost had left his mark.

"There are dirty dishes in the kitchen sink, too. How about the bedrooms?" Marty asked. "The least he could have done was put his dirty dishes in the dishwasher."

"Don't touch anything! We're going to have enough to account for as it is by roaming around down here without a police escort." It's more likely that if we'd reported the opening, we would have been told to leave so we wouldn't have been allowed down here at all.

"Yep!" Carl replied as he returned from checking the bedrooms. "Shakespeare was here! Go see for yourselves, if you want to. That's where Danny De Voss donned his costume, and there's a spare wig, plus makeup and who knows what else in there." Then, he scanned the suite. "There's real plumbing in this place—unlike a bomb shelter. All the comforts of home if you had to wait out a police manhunt before you could put the passageways to good use as an escape route."

"Hank is going to want to send a team down here. Maybe there's evidence about who killed Shakespeare," Charly said as we exited the suite.

"Or where," Neely said pointing to a spot we'd passed earlier. In the light from the open door, we could see smears of white greasepaint on the floor and wall not far from the foot of the stairs we'd traipsed down. A few drops of what appeared to be dried blood were also on the floor.

"I'm so glad we didn't step in it," Marty said. "That's disgusting."

"You have more than that to be grateful for. Can you imagine the tongue-lashing we'd get from Devers if we'd done that? Even though we found secret passageways that he would never have found because he would have dismissed the idea as crazy."

"Why don't we break up into teams of two and check out as much of this underground network as we can in another twenty minutes or so? Then we'll go back upstairs and call Hank," Charly suggested. We were going to pay a price for roaming around down here like a small herd of lost sheep. On the other hand, we'd not only found our way into the underground complex as Midge pointed out, but we'd located the place where Danny De Voss had been attacked. Suddenly, the hair on the back of my neck stood up.

"Keeping our visit short appeals to me. If Danny De Voss was stabbed down here, his killer knows about these passageways, too."

"I agree. I want get an idea of where the other corridors lead while we're down here," Joe said.

"Don't go too far, especially if it leads to another crossroad and you're tempted to make another turn or two or three. Once you start making choices about which way to go in the dim light, it'll be too easy to lose track of where you are."

"If you take the first passageway," Midge said, "Marty and I will take the next one."

"We will?" Marty asked.

"Hang on a second," I said. Without further explanation, I ran back into the storage room and grabbed a bunch of big thick markers I'd seen in there. When I returned, I passed them out. "Before you head down a corridor, mark it with a big X or a black dot. Then, if you get lost, we have a chance of tracking you even if you can't use the marks to backtrack and find your way out."

"That's as good as bread crumbs. I like that!" Neely exclaimed. "Robyn and I will take the third passageway."

"There are probably bread crumbs in there, too," I said. "I could look if you'd prefer to leave that kind of a trail to follow back."

"No!" Robyn asserted. "What if there are rats down here and the bread crumbs draw them out? I don't trust myself not to panic and run. I'd be lost in no time."

"We'll all meet back here in twenty minutes. That means we'll give ourselves ten minutes out with ten minutes to get back. Miriam and I are going to put on the speed and not stop to look at anything along the way. I want to see if we can find where this main passageway ends." With that, we all took off at a clip. Teams peeled off as we came to each of the first three corridors which seemed to be spaced about a block apart. It was tempting to peek into the nooks and crannies we passed, but I resisted given the goal we'd set.

That worked fine until I smelled mildew, dirt, and something rotten. Charly and I both stopped when we saw chunks of cement, rocks, and dirt in the corridor ahead of us. When we got closer, it was clear that part of the structure to our right had given way and lay in a pile of rubble. I couldn't see daylight, but I caught a shred of bright orange webbing in the beam of my flashlight when I probed the breach in the wall. It was mixed in with more debris near the top of the rubble.

"Oh, yuck," I said as I stepped back quickly.

"What is it?" Charly asked.

"More bones, including a skull with its eyes staring straight at me."

"Skulls can't stare." Then she stopped speaking. "It isn't a pleasant sight, though, is it?"

"No. This might give members of the forensics team an easier way to claim those stinky old bones, though, than going in from above." Just then, I felt a whoosh of cool air pass through my hair and around my neck before it moved along the side of my face. I reached up and touched my cheek. It's as if something cool and clammy had touched me. A few more rocks and more dirt slid down and spilled out onto our path.

"Did you feel that?" I asked.

"Feel what? The rocks tumbling?"

"No. I don't know—never mind. I hope this place is structurally sound, don't you?"

"It seems pretty sturdy elsewhere. A big quake might shake things up, but what are the odds?"

"How would I know that?" I asked with my voice starting to sound a little whiny. "Let's finish the task we promised to do and then get out of here."

"At least we have an idea of how far we've come. A few more blocks and we'll be near the clubhouse." She tore off, and I had to jog to catch up with her. "Another few blocks beyond that will take us outside our community. What if this corridor goes all the way to the old Hempstead Towers outbuildings that have been preserved?"

"Exiting from down here into an old barn or stable

would be one way to climb up out of the ground without being seen. I suppose even now that the property has been declared a historical site, that wouldn't deter Ted De Voss from treating it as if he still owned it."

We were moving at top speed now. Twenty years older than me, Charly was in excellent condition. I didn't mind. The image of the skull kept coming back to me, along with the memory of that cold, moist blast of air.

"What if that was Cookie De Voss looking at me back there?" I asked. "Why would the killer have buried her there?"

"I was wondering about that last night. I'm pretty sure the golf course wasn't installed here until the seventies. You can probably get the date by searching the archives. If they were installing the irrigation system and whatever else went into the ground with it, why not stash her dead body in a shallow grave in a field that was already churned up?"

"Well, she deserves a better resting place than that—done wrong in life and in death—that's a double injustice."

"I agree." We'd covered a lot of ground as we spoke, although I was now breathing so hard, I was no longer interested in chatting. I thought I felt the ground shake above us.

"Cars driving above us," Charly commented and pressed on.

I lit the corridor ahead of us with my flashlight, checking the walls and the roof, as well as the path underfoot. We'd gone about another block when my beam picked up the gleam of metal. A metal stair rail and stairs led up to the surface. When we got closer, I stopped in my tracks. Something dead ahead moved.

17

Strange Bedfellows

"Misery acquaints a man with strange bedfellows."

—The Tempest

∞

"**W**HAT WAS THAT?**"** Charly asked in a whisper. "I'm glad you noticed it. I was afraid I was seeing things."

"I don't see or hear anybody. Let's take a closer look, then we've got to head back, or we'll be late for our rendezvous." We walked a little closer with both of our flashlights on the wall ahead of us. We'd clearly come to the end of the road.

Upon closer inspection, it was also clear that what rose up in front of us was another point of entry and exit. Although it was painted to match the surrounding rock wall, we were staring at a door. A big one that could have allowed someone to drive that forklift in here. What had moved was a scrap of something caught in the door near the cement floor.

"I'm not going to touch it or move it. There's a small

branch of bougainvillea caught in the door. Someone tracked this in here recently because the leaves aren't faded and dried out yet. There's also part of a narrow tire track near it."

"Maybe Shakespeare or his killer rode in and out of here on a motorbike or scooter. There's enough room, anywhere along the route, to turn around on one of those. I only remember seeing one or two places big enough for the forklift or anything as large as a golf cart to do that."

"I haven't smelled gasoline or exhaust, have you?" I asked.

"No, but there must be some reason this entire area doesn't stink like a basement. When we passed some of the corridors, I felt cross breezes."

"I did, too—ocean breezes. I don't know how that's possible, but this is a place with mysteries that could take a lifetime to unravel."

"Let's get back to the others. We're already going to be late." Charly was right about that. We hadn't gone far before we heard the rumbling of motors and saw head-lights in the distance coming toward us.

"I hope they're on our side. I'm going to signal them, so we don't get run over." I flicked the beam on my flashlight on and off a few times. We got a response back. When they got closer, a minute or two later, they slowed.

"Charly's Angels, to the rescue!" Joe exclaimed.

"Thanks, Joe," I replied.

"Hop on, and we'll take you back." Charly didn't hesi-tate, but I wasn't sure the motorbike could accommodate two people. When Charly settled in behind Joe, I did the same on the bike Carl rode.

Somehow, I squeezed on, and we sped away. In minutes, we were back with the rest of our crew. They had no trouble seeing us coming because someone had found a way to light the area near the stairs leading from the cottage.

"Where did you find these?" I asked as I climbed off the motorbike.

"There were several of them in an alcove off the corridor we explored," Carl replied.

"That's not all. We saw all kinds of stuff in there. Some of it's old, right Carl?"

"Yes. The older stuff was farther away. You were right to tell us not to make unmarked turns, Charly. It's like a maze once you leave the main corridor. The markers worked fine for the first couple of turns and then the cement walls ended. It's dirt after that." They stashed the motorbikes out of the way as Neely chimed in.

"The corridor we were in sloped down toward the beach. We followed some of the twists and turns. It felt like we were inside an anthill. The turns make it easy to lose track of the direction in which you're moving. We didn't have to use the felt tip pen. Someone had left arrows for us to follow so we could find our way back to where we'd started. The cement floors gave way to dirt, as well as the walls."

"When we hit dirt, that was it for me," Robyn added.

"We ran into a little dirt along the way, too." Charly explained that we'd found an underground route to the sinkhole the dogs had played in the day before.

"We also found more bones and a skull," I added. I'm sure if I'd kept silent, Charly would have mentioned it. For some reason, I suddenly felt the need to wrap this up.

"We didn't find motorbikes, but someone left this light in a crevice cut into the dirt wall," Midge said.

"I wouldn't go down any of those passageways without a flashlight, that's for sure. I'll bet Danny De Voss has been all through there if he's been treasure hunting. I wonder if he found the note that he had with him when he was killed down here somewhere."

"No one would have tried to stop him from doing whatever he wanted for as long as he wanted," Carl added.

"If that note isn't the only clue he found, someone may have stopped Danny from claiming the treasure, though. Why not leave the note behind if they killed him to get him to give them something else that was better than that?" Neely asked.

"Well, if what's going on in the cottage has anything to do with the smuggling ring, we didn't stumble across any evidence of it. No fake Gucci purses or Givenchy shoes— nothing to suggest the smugglers were stashing counterfeit goods down here."

"It could be done. Miriam and I didn't climb the stairs to confirm that the exit at the end of the main corridor opens to a ramp that leads up into the old Hempstead Towers barn. I'm guessing that's about where it would be, though, given the distance we covered. The door we found is big enough to allow forklifts to haul stuff in here."

"I can't understand storing stuff down here for very long. In a jam, it would work as a place to ditch the goods. There must be miles of passageways to search. Unless the smugglers drew them a map, the police would never find where they'd hidden the goods."

"Carl's right about that," Robyn said. "Even if they got hold of a map, all you'd have to do is come down here and move it." Midge was playing with the switch on the light she held, getting antsy or nervous.

"That's a black light, isn't it?" I asked.

"It sure is—a professional one like crime scene investigators use," Midge responded. "It'll pick up bodily fluids that have been left behind at the scene of a crime."

"Lights like that can also read invisible ink if the smugglers are leaving secret messages for each other down here. The spy technique's no longer in vogue the way it was during most of the major wars in U.S. history, starting with George Washington," Charly said. "Still, a group of Russian spies exposed in 2010 was using it. UV lights can read anything written using an organic fluid like blood or urine, but other ordinary substances like lemon juice."

"I've got one of those to make sure Scheherazade can't hide her mistakes from me," Marty offered.

"I get it," I said not wanting any more details than that. Something about the idea nagged at me though. The concept was intriguing—using invisible ink to hide the truth in plain sight.

"We didn't find anything of much value, although some of the junk piled up in places might be of interest to collectors. There's a box of old bottles that must have come from the De Voss family misadventures during Prohibition. If it's Depression-era glass, Marty says that'll bring in a few bucks if you can find the right collector," Midge said.

"It makes sense that part of this network was built

back then and connected to the old house before it was torn down," I said.

"There were a few places that had odd markings—like cave paintings. Stones are laid out in patterns on the ground or embedded in the walls. Now that I'm talking about it, my skin is getting goosebumps. If Daniel and Constance were into occult practices, I can't imagine a creepier place to practice them than in that network of passageways."

"As stoned as Daniel De Voss was, it's amazing he didn't get lost down here," Joe commented. "Maybe that's why no one knows where the family vault is—they lost it down here. Whoever wrote that note must still be laughing even if he's long dead. It's too bad walls can't talk," Joe said. "Treasure hunting and sleuthing sure works up an appetite. Let's get out of here and go see what Chef Tony has on the menu for lunch."

"What if walls can talk?" I asked. "If the handwriting is on the wall, you might not be able to hear it, but you could sure see it. Especially if the Great Wall gives up its secrets." I hustled over to the storage room, went in, and picked up a picture Neely and I'd noticed earlier. I brought it back to the others. The vibrant painting tagged: **The Great Southern Wall of Isengard**, was signed in one corner by D. B. De Voss. It was dated '71.

"It's one of Tolkien's valleys," Neely said without hesitation.

"Signed by Daniel Bradley De Voss," Charly added. "Ted De Voss's dead brother the same year he died."

"Given what a stoner and hippy he was, it's not surprising he painted something from Tolkien, is it?" Joe asked. "I don't see any handwriting on the wall, either. Can we go eat, now?"

"I want to try something, and then we can go. Pass me the black light, will you Midge?" I propped the painting against the door of the storage room.

"Sure."

"Here goes nothing," I whispered as I turned the black light on and swept the surface of the painting. At first, I didn't see a thing. Then, Neely, who has the poorest sight among us, gasped.

"How do you like that—an invisible drawing on the painting? The great wall in Daniel's painting has given up its secrets. If you hold the light steady, you can see that's a map of the tunnels with the location of the vault marked on it in Roman numerals," she said. Then she gazed at me. "How much do you want to bet those numbers are a combination for the vault?" Suddenly, we heard slow, rhythmic clapping. When we all turned away from the painting, we stood there with our mouths gaping.

"'Misery acquaints a man with strange bedfellows,' doesn't it?" Midge asked. None of us could bring ourselves to respond when the gun pointing at us took aim at Midge.

18

Foregone Conclusion

"But this denoted a foregone conclusion."
—Othello

∞

"**S**HUT UP AND step away from the painting," Eddie Vargas ordered as he shifted his aim again, and settled on Carl as his target. He also moved toward us as he issued that command. We all did as he asked, although I edged backward, not away from the painting. If he noticed, he didn't show it. When his co-conspirator distracted him, I scooted even a little closer to the painting.

"You'd better do as he says!" Bernie De Voss shrieked as she moved down the stairs and stood next to the detective. "He's even handier with a gun than he is with a knife."

"No!" Marty gasped. "If you're saying Eddie Vargas killed your son, don't you care?"

"Danny wasn't my son. I can't believe you nosy snoops didn't figure that out. Cookie was his mom."

"Even if he was Cookie's son, instead of yours, doesn't

that matter to you?" Charly asked in a calm, steady voice.

"Why? Cookie De Voss took everything from me! Daniel was supposed to marry me. He would have, too, until she seduced him and then told him she was pregnant. He believed her, too, when she said he was the baby's father." Bernie was shaking with emotion.

"Wasn't he?" I asked suddenly overwhelmed by curiosity. As Eddie and Bernie glared at me, Charly inched closer to Eddie.

"No, he was not. He was Ted's son. Why else would my husband's first marriage have ended so soon? It killed Daniel when Ted told him the truth. Ted wouldn't stop until he got his hands on what was his, not that he ever cared about his son once he claimed him. Daniel was a sweet, gentle soul, and those two ripped his heart out."

"A sweet, gentle soul who was trafficking and dealing drugs. That's a new one," Midge said in a disgusted tone.

"Don't say that! Kill her, Eddie. She gets to be the first to die."

"Like Cookie De Voss, you mean?" Charly asked. "We found her, although I'm afraid her resting place isn't going to remain a secret much longer. Did you kill her or did her sweet, gentle husband do that?"

"Stop it! I wasn't even around here until after she disappeared, and Daniel would never have done that. You can't believe a word Ted tells you. He's a monster." Bernie dissolved into tears.

"Why did you marry a monster?" I asked.

"I didn't understand any of this at first, and decided that even if I couldn't have Daniel, I could raise his son. I stayed with Ted, year after year, just to keep Danny safe, especially once he and Ted refused to see each other anymore. I covered for Danny when he visited me. When Ted found out that Danny and I were still close, he wanted to hurt me. That's when he told me what he'd done to Cookie. Once I knew where she was buried, I couldn't live here anymore. That's also when I noticed things were being moved. At first, I thought Ted was doing it to drive me mad, but even when he was gone for months, it continued. I begged Ted to buy a house in Santa Barbara and rent the cottage."

"Aw, come on. Cookie De Voss had plenty of reason to haunt you, but that was your son—sorry—Ted's son, sneaking around here looking for the family vault, wasn't it? You must know that." Bernie glared at Neely before she spoke in an eerily controlled voice, still seething with rage.

"Yes, I do, thanks to Eddie. Danny didn't care about me anymore than the other De Voss men." Bernie nudged Eddie toward us. "Now, she gets to be first to die. Start shooting, Eddie. What are you waiting for? No one can hear us down here."

"You're really going to kill all of us?" Neely asked. "Aren't there enough restless souls roaming these empty corridors?" As she said that, the cold, clammy breeze that had hit me before, swirled around us. It was tinged with a hint of the terrible odor that had come from the site where that skull had gaped at me, wide-eyed and open-mouthed.

"No one's going to die unless you force my hand," Eddie said. All we want is that painting, and then we'll leave. Your lives are a parting gift for helping us figure out where the vault's located. Whatever else he was, Ted's brother, Daniel was clever. Bernie tells me that before his parents shipped him off to boarding school, her first love spent much of his childhood exploring these passageways. I figured he must have had a map to find his way around down here, or the flake would have gotten lost."

"Danny was the same way until Ted sent him away to school. When he came back, I couldn't understand his renewed fascination with this place until he told me that Daniel had left him a note about how to find a hidden family fortune. It made sense to me that there was some truth to what he said. I'd never seen some of Daniel's favorite artwork or artifacts. They weren't in storage, either, because I checked. Ted finally admitted Daniel had stolen them and that's what had provoked the crisis with Cookie and Daniel. Neither one of them would tell him what Daniel had done with the family treasures he'd stolen and hidden."

"Stolen is right—not all of them by Daniel, either. The family's love of other people's property goes as far back as their interest in smuggling. When I asked Danny to cooperate with the latest investigation, he had no problem acting as an informant to help put his dad behind bars if I agreed to let him keep searching down here. I didn't get it, so I offered Bernie a similar deal, and she told me about Danny's obsession with the fortune."

"Which is when you sold out and decided to go for the gold yourself," Joe commented. Eddie's trigger finger wiggled ever so slightly as Joe became his new target.

"He's my candidate for the first to die. How about it, Bernie? That guy and his buddy came close to blowing the whole investigation wide open and putting me in a very bad spot! Especially when they had Mickey cornered."

"I know you didn't want to kill Mickey, even though he let you down and didn't pick up Danny for you as you asked. I doubt it would have mattered since Danny said he'd found the paining that held the key to the riddle, but I doubt he'd figured out the invisible ink angle or he and his fortune would have been long gone."

"He must have figured it out since we found the black light down here. If not, it was only a matter of time before he did and led you to the treasure. Given what a great friend he considered you to be, Eddie, he might even have shared his good fortune with you—like George says you're going to do with him, Bernie."

"Said." Bernie fixed me with a withering glance. I must have looked as horrified as I felt. "Quit worrying about my witless cousin, George. He's no longer worrying about anything. He did his part to see that Ted's going to get what he has coming to him for killing Cookie. Not that George will get any credit for it. Eddie's fixed it so that George and Mickey will take the blame for all the recent trouble around here. Unfortunately, they killed each other over a squabble about smuggled goods they'd swiped from Ted. The knife that killed Danny is in George's cold, dead hand."

"Don't feel too sorry for Danny either. He wasn't going to share anything with us. Talk about witless! He suddenly got the bright idea to tell Ted about the note and the painting, if you can believe that. I tried to convince Danny he was never going to show his dad up, or be the big hero by restoring the lost family fortune to a man who didn't care about him in the first place. Besides, Ted's about to be arrested and everything he owns will be seized and forfeited. Danny wouldn't listen to reason and he had to be stopped."

"Don't you see why we've got to get our hands on whatever's in that vault and get out of here with it?" Bernie asked with desperation in her eyes.

"She's right. Time is one thing Bernie and I don't have, folks. Nor do you. If you're stalling because you believe Hank Miller is on his way, forget about it. He's got his hands full already, as you can imagine, with two more dead bodies. I'm the point person on the cottage today."

I knew Eddie was lying about letting us all go, or he and Bernie wouldn't have been so verbose about what they'd done to George Pierson and Mickey Paulson. Maybe now that he had the map, he'd use it to lead us into the web of corridors and leave us there to die.

That wasn't going to happen. The great wall had given up its secrets—to us. I didn't intend to let Eddie get his hands on the painting even if I had to destroy it. I made eye contact with Charly as I slowly slid my hand toward the closest corner of the painting.

"Time's up, folks. I'm not going to kill anybody, but how about a new knee for Joe?" As he pointed the gun at Joe, I grabbed the painting and gouged it with a fingernail, with my fingers poised to do more damage.

"Put the gun down, or I'll scrape off more paint before you can shoot any of us and the map to the vault will be gone." He turned the gun on me, and with his free hand he made a grab for the painting. As he did that, Charly whipped out her kubotan, and using it as a flail hit his hand hard enough to draw blood. The gun flew out of his hand and Bernie scrambled to get it. Without a flashlight handy, I hit her with the edge of the painting instead. Charly had Eddie Vargas in a jiu-jitsu hold, so Carl and Joe grabbed Bernie, while Marty picked up the gun.

"What on earth made you believe you could take down our entire gang?" Midge asked. "If you'd paid more attention to Shakespeare, you might have realized it was a foregone conclusion that you couldn't outwit the Grand Old Lady Detectives and Charly's Angels." Eddie Vargas and Bernie De Voss just stood there gawking. I'm sure little of what Midge had just said made a lick of sense to them. These two were no fans of Shakespeare, that's for sure.

∞

IT DIDN'T TAKE Hank long to arrive once I'd gone upstairs and called 911. I was so relieved that when Hank reached the bottom of those stairs, I threw myself into his arms. My words tumbled over each other as I tried to explain what had gone on and all that we'd learned. Eddie Vargas and Bernie De Voss who'd been so virulently expressive while Eddie was armed, stood as mum and motionless as statues.

I hadn't realized it at the time, but I was drenched in sweat. When another of those odd, cold clammy breezes blew around me, it lingered longer than it had before and then left me chilled to the bone. There was a delicate sweetness in the scent it carried—a hint of gardenia, perhaps. I was shivering, and one of the EMTs who'd responded to the 911 call draped a blanket around my shoulders.

"Did you feel it this time?" I asked Charly. She nodded yes as she gratefully accepted a blanket, too. "What was it?"

"An uneasy spirit set free, maybe."

"You don't really mean that, do you?"

"'*There are more things in heaven and earth, Miriam, than are dreamt of in your philosophy.*' Who am I to argue with Shakespeare? Seaview Cottages is full of spirits. That's why we're drawn here, and why we stay. We conjure them up every time we utter a dead writer's name. I'm not talking about comic book or horror story versions of ghosts and goblins. If you believe in any kind of an afterlife, you must feel better considering the possibility that their genius, foibles and all, still exists somewhere. Even your poor, desperate Hemingway." On some level, I sensed she was right. Or maybe it was more a matter of hope. In any case, I couldn't imagine her bright spirit ever yielding to anything—not even death.

"So, let's go get this settled, clean ourselves up, and feed Joe."

"Sounds good to me. Then we can come back and find the paintings and artifacts Bernie says Daniel De Voss hid now that we have the map and the combination to the vault. I can't wait to see what's in the family vault."

"Oh, no you don't," Hank said. "The feds are going to be all over this place any minute. They're very interested in what's in the vault. It's evidence, even if some of it is priceless. Who knows how many crimes they'll solve once they inventory everything Daniel De Voss hid in the vault? That's especially true if you all stay out of there!"

"Will you at least tell us what they find?" Marty asked.

"I'll do my best. I promise," Hank replied. Joe seemed let down, but I was too tired to care as we trudged up the steps, into the pantry, and left the Shakespeare Cottage. Then I remembered something Charly had mentioned in passing. As we were all huddled together on the porch, I asked her about it.

"As I recall, you mentioned that we have another client, right?" I saw weary faces perk up.

"We do. A cold case, like Cookie De Voss. Perhaps, another restless soul seeking justice. An old friend of mine, Judith Rogow, has asked us to find her son's grave on Dickens' Dune.

—THE END—

Thanks for reading *The Murder of Shakespeare's Ghost* Seaview Cottages Cozy Mystery #2. I hope you'll take a minute to leave me a review on Amazon, Bookbub, and Goodreads. Follow me, too, on Amazon bit.ly/acburke. Subscribe to my email for news about books, discounts, giveaways, and special events: desertcitiesmystery.com.

What's next for Miriam and her friends? Their next case, of course, and Miriam has a new secret—one she didn't know she was keeping. To find out more, grab your copy of *Grave Expectations on Dickens' Dune* Seaview Cottages Cozy Mystery #3. Here's the blurb!

Sometimes the most dangerous secrets are the ones we don't know we're keeping.

A cold case doesn't stay cold for long when Miriam and her Grand Old Lady Detective [G.O.L.D.] pals take on a new mystery to solve. Charly's old friend, Judith Rogow, asks for her help in locating her ex-husband's grave. A veteran of the Vietnam War, Allen Rogow survived the war and returned home, only to disappear several years later. Although evidence pointed to murder, the police never found his body.

When an ex-convict makes a deathbed confession, he claims someone murdered Allen Rogow because of a secret he promised to carry to his grave. Did someone make sure he kept his promise and is he buried in an unmarked grave on Dickens' Dune? Is Allen Rogow's killer still alive and intent on making sure no one unearths the truth?

As the cold case warms up, it turns out Allen Rogow wasn't the only person keeping a dangerous secret. Miriam has a new one too—courtesy of her dead husband's hidden life.

Grab your copy of book 3 in the Seaview Cottages Cozy Mystery series by USA Today and Wall Street Journal bestselling author, Anna Celeste Burke. Join Miriam, the entire G.O.L.D. team, and Charly's Angels as they try to discover what the dickens is going on in *Grave Expectations on Dickens' Dune*.

Recipes Included.

Free to read with Kindle Unlimited.

There's more fun, food, and mystery coming soon with G.O.L.D. and Charly's Angels. In the meantime, I hope you'll have a chance to try out a recipe or two from the dishes featured in this book. Enjoy!

RECIPES

Strawberry Cake
About 16 Servings

Ingredients

<u>Cake</u>
2 cups self-rising flour
2 cups sugar
4 eggs
1 teaspoon vanilla
2 teaspoons lemon juice
1 cup canola or coconut oil
1 cup milk
1/4 cup sweetened strawberries, mashed
1 small box strawberry gelatin

<u>Icing</u>
2 cups sliced strawberries
1 cup butter, softened
3 cups confectioners' sugar
1 teaspoon vanilla extract

Preparation
Preheat oven to 350 degrees F.

Mix all cake ingredients and pour into greased 9×13 pan. Bake at 350 degrees for 25–30 minutes or until toothpick comes out clean.

While the cake bakes, prepare the icing.
Mix together all icing ingredients until smooth. Add more powdered sugar, if needed. Icing should be spreadable but not runny.

Once the cake is cool, spread the icing on the cake. Refrigerate for at least two hours. Serve chilled.

Baked Macaroni and Cheese
Serves 4–5

Ingredients
3 tablespoons unsalted butter
2 tablespoons flour
12 ounces canned evaporated milk
1/2 cup half and half
1/4 teaspoon cayenne pepper
1/2 teaspoon paprika
1/2 cup mozzarella cheese, grated
1 cup sharp cheddar cheese, grated
1/2 cup jack cheese, grated
Salt and pepper to taste
8 ounces uncooked macaroni

Preparation
Preheat oven to 375 degrees F.

Cook the macaroni according to the package directions. Drain well.

Add butter to skillet. As soon as the butter melts, whisk in flour until flour is fully mixed with butter. Then cook for about a minute to get rid of the flour taste.

Slowly add evaporated milk a little at a time. Then add the half and half and whisk until the mixture is smooth. Simmer for about 3–5 minutes until the mixture thickens slightly.

Add cayenne pepper and simmer for another 2 minutes.

Reserve 1/2 cup cheddar for topping. Stir in the rest of the cheese and continue stirring until cheese is melted and the sauce is smooth. Salt and pepper, to taste.

Add the cooked pasta to the pot and stir to coat it in the cheese sauce.

Pour the pasta mixture into a lightly greased 2-quart baking dish. Top with the remaining cheddar cheese.

Bake for 20 minutes or until golden and bubbly.

Beef Tenderloin with Red Wine, Anchovies, Garlic, and Herbs
Serves 8

Ingredients

4 tablespoons unsalted butter (1/2 stick), cut 2 tablespoons into small dice and chilled

2 tablespoons extra-virgin olive oil

8 shallots, sliced or minced

Kosher salt

2 teaspoons fresh thyme leaves

1 teaspoon fresh oregano

8 garlic cloves, peeled and crushed with the flat side of a chef's knife

12 anchovy fillets packed in olive oil, drained and minced

2 pieces beef tenderloin, 1 1/2 pounds each, trimmed and cleaned

Fresh ground black pepper

2 teaspoons sugar

1/4 cup brandy

1 1/4 cups good quality red wine

Fresh arugula, for serving

Preparation

Place the beef tenderloins in a large, heavy-bottomed pot in which they fit without touching each other or the sides of the pot. Before cooking the meat, heat 2 tablespoons butter and 1 tablespoon of oil over low heat. Add the shallots, sprinkle with a little salt, and sauté until soft and transparent, about 5 minutes. Add the thyme and oregano and cook for 2 more minutes, then add the garlic and mix with the other ingredients.

Add the anchovies and cook until they disintegrate, virtually melting into the rest of the ingredients. Pour the mixture into a bowl.

Add the remaining tablespoon of oil to the pot and turn up the heat. Pat the beef dry and season it with salt and pepper. Sear the beef on all sides, while sprinkling with the sugar to get a crusty exterior. Carefully, add the brandy making sure it doesn't come into contact with an open flame! Let it simmer until it bubbles and then add the wine.

Return the shallot mixture to the pot. Lower the heat and turn the meat over. Stir so the shallots mixture doesn't stick or burn. Cover and cook for 10 minutes.

After ten minutes, uncover and check the meat. If it's springy to the touch, it's rare. If that's the way you want to eat and serve it, remove the meat. If you prefer medium rare—still springy but with some resistance, turn the meat over, cover and cook for about five minutes longer or closer to ten minutes for medium. When the meat is close to the way you want it (it will cook a little more as it rests), transfer to a cutting board. While the meat rests finish the sauce.

Fish out the garlic from the pot with a spoon. Then turn up the heat and let the sauce bubble. Taste it and add salt, if needed, and pepper. You may want to thin it with a little water. Take it off the heat, add the meat juices from the cooked beef, stir in the remaining chilled, diced butter, and serve immediately.

To serve, slice the beef, arrange it on a plate surrounded with arugula. Drizzle a little sauce over the meat. Put the rest in a sauce boat for guests to pour for themselves.

Baked Ziti with Vegetables
4 servings

Ingredients
8 ounces uncooked ziti pasta
2 tablespoon olive oil
2 cups chopped yellow squash
1 cup chopped zucchini
1/2 cup chopped red onion
2 cups sliced cherry tomatoes
2 garlic cloves, minced
1 cup part skim milk mozzarella, shredded
1/4 cup ricotta cheese
1/4 cup grated Romano cheese
2 tablespoons chopped fresh basil
2 teaspoons chopped fresh oregano
3/4 teaspoon salt
1/8 teaspoon cayenne
1 large egg, beaten

Preparation
Cook pasta according to the directions—about 10 minutes. Drain and set aside.

Preheat broiler while the pasta is cooking. Place oven rack 6 inches from heat. Toss squash, zucchini, tomatoes, onion, garlic, 1 tablespoon olive oil, 1/2 teaspoon salt, and then spread on a foil-lined rimmed baking sheet in a single layer; broil until browned and tender, about 10 minutes.

Preheat oven to 400 degrees F.

Stir together Romano cheese, ricotta cheese, egg, 1/4 teaspoon salt, basil, oregano, and cayenne

Combine vegetables, pasta, 1/2 cup mozzarella and spoon half into the bottom of a two-quart baking dish that's been coated with cooking spray. Drop spoonfuls of the ricotta and Romano cheese mixture, using half. Then create another layer using the pasta and veggie mixture, then topping with remaining Romano and ricotta cheese mixture. Top with the remaining half cup of shredded mozzarella.

Bake for 15 minutes until brown and bubbly. Let stand 5 minutes before serving.

Triple Ginger Cookies

About three dozen cookies

Ingredients

2 1/2 cups all-purpose flour

1/2 cup minced crystallized ginger

2 teaspoons baking soda

1/4 teaspoon salt

3/4 cup (1 1/2 sticks) unsalted butter, room temperature

1/2 cup packed golden brown sugar

1/2 cup packed dark brown sugar

1 large egg, room temperature

1/4 cup light, mild-flavored molasses

2 teaspoons finely grated fresh peeled ginger

1 1/2 teaspoons ground ginger

1 teaspoon ground cinnamon

1/2 teaspoon ground cloves

1/3 cup granulated sugar

Preparation

Preheat to 350 degrees F.

Line 2 baking sheets with parchment paper.

Whisk together flour, crystallized ginger, baking soda, and 1/4 teaspoon salt in medium bowl.

In a separate large bowl, use an electric mixer, beat butter until creamy. Gradually add both brown sugars and beat on medium-high until creamy, about 3 minutes. Add egg, molasses, fresh ginger, ground ginger, cinnamon, and cloves, and blend well.

Add flour mixture in thirds, beating on low speed just to blend between additions.

Place 1/3 cup sugar in small bowl. Measure 1 tablespoon dough. Roll into ball between palms of hands, then roll in sugar in bowl to coat; place on baking sheet. Repeat with remaining cookie dough, spacing cookies 1 1/2 to 2 inches apart.

Bake cookies until surfaces crack and cookies are firm around edges but still slightly soft in center, about 15 minutes. Cool completely still on the baking sheets. Cookies can be stored in airtight containers at room temperature.

About the Author

An award-winning, USA Today and Wall Street Journal bestselling author, I hope you'll join me *snooping into life's mysteries with fun, fiction, and food—California style!*

Life is an extravaganza! Figuring out how to hang tough and make the most of the wild ride is the challenge. On my way to Oahu, to join the rock musician and high school drop-out I had married in Tijuana, I was nabbed as a runaway. Eventually, the police let me go, but the rock band broke up.

Retired now, I'm still married to the same sweet guy and live with him near Palm Springs, California. I write the Jessica Huntington Desert Cities Mystery series set here in the Coachella Valley, the Corsario Cove Cozy Mystery Series set along California's Central Coast, The Georgie Shaw Mystery series set in the OC, The Seaview Cottages Cozy Mystery Series set on the so-called American Riviera, just north of Santa Barbara, and The Calla Lily Mystery series where the murder and mayhem take place in California's Wine Country. Won't you join me? Sign up at: desertcitiesmystery.com.